RETURN TO SENDER

A MAIL CARRIER COZY MYSTERY BOOK 4

TONYA KAPPES

CHAPTER 1

Benefits of yoga: energy regulations. Yeah, I was still waiting on that one. Stronger bones. If that was the case, why did Doctor Hunter give me supplements to take on my last well-woman visit because my bone density test recorded early osteoporosis?

I groaned as my hands rotated up to warrior two pose. Helped you focus, yeah right. The sarcasm was so loud in my head that I had to look around to see if anyone heard it.

"Bernie." The soft whisper of Peaches Partin circled the space above everyone's warrior pose in the beginning yoga class that Iris Peabody had insisted we take. "Focus by looking down your arm and past your fingertips."

Was that Peaches's way of telling me to stop looking around? Mmhmmm... which brings me to another reason I was given to try yoga: increased happiness. The only thing bringing me happiness was the fact I was going to be able to watch Clara, my granddaughter, this afternoon while Julia, my daughter-in-law, went to the doctor for her checkup.

Which brought me to the next reason I was given: helping me sleep. That wasn't working. I was always up at night worrying if my premature granddaughter was thriving or how her early birth was going to impact her growth. I loved her no matter what, but it was really the stress I'd seen on Julia's and my son, Grady's, faces that always told me they only wanted the best for little Clara.

Apparently, focusing down my arm made me a little wobbly, which sent Peaches right on over to steady me.

"I thought this was supposed to give me good balance?" I asked her.

Iris Peabody laughed. Peaches didn't find it a bit funny.

"Focus," Peaches whispered and gently let go like I was a kite about to take off in a gentle wind, only to me it felt like a tornado.

Which brought me to another reason I was sold on the whole idea of yoga: improved muscle strength. I'd like to see it. The only muscle strength I'd gotten was sore, achy, and spasmodic, not to mention how much ibuprofen I'd purchased since I'd let Iris talk me into this crazy activity.

I was a walking mail carrier. I walked miles upon miles a day. By the end of the day, my feet did ache, but nothing a good Epsom salt foot soak didn't take care of. And I'd started to go over to Jenny Franklin's since I'd heard she'd been doing hair and nails in her basement.

She sure did give a good foot rub along with a bang-up toenail paint job. Plus, I liked to help out the small business owners in the area.

My stomach gurgled. A little belch drew up into my esophagus, reminding me what I'd eaten at midnight while worrying about my granddaughter. This brought me to the two final reasons I'd decided to let Iris talk me into contorting my fifty-year-old body in ways that shouldn't be twisted.

Yoga helped with your digestion. Now, keep in mind that Iris was the owner of Pie in the Face, the local bakery. Not only the proprietor, but the baker. And to beat the band, she suggested this yoga class over a freshly baked maple walnut crumb cake that just so happened to be surrounded in cinnamon, walnuts, and brown sugar with brown sugar crumbles on top. And I couldn't forget to mention how it was also smothered in a vanilla bean Vermont maple glaze that was to die for.

We would both gobble up a much larger piece than we needed of the delicious sweet-baked good with a big cup of ice-cold milk to wash it down.

Yoga helped you lose weight. I slid my eyes down to my gut that had started to become a little rounder than it'd been in years past.

My eyes moved across the room as Peaches told us to move to reverse warrior. Lucy Drake's thin, streamlined body fit perfectly in her fancy yoga pants and sleeveless formfitting top. The Tranquility Wellness water bottle Peaches sold with the logo on it was sitting half-empty on the floor next to her hot-pink yoga mat.

Her long hair flowed down her back, making her a stark resemblance to the poster on the wall promoting a new yoga wear line Peaches sold in the Tranquility Wellness shop. I pushed back my stick-straight auburn hair, pretending it didn't look like a big grease pit. Though in the back of my head, I knew from the long day of walking and sweating that I didn't look as fresh as Lucy.

"Last rose of summer," I moaned as I tried to sink deeper into the pose Peaches was telling everyone to do.

"What?" Iris asked, staring forward.

"Nothing." I looked down at my wobbling thighs, begging them not to collapse under me. Then I made the mistake of using my peripheral vision to see Lucy Drake, stiff and holding her pose as though she was a goddess statue.

I bet a big old juicy hamburger and large fry from supper

last night wasn't sitting in her gut like a big brick like it was mine. Her stomach was nice and flat. Everything about her wanted me to snarl and gnash my teeth. Her good looks, her popularity from hosting her own morning radio show on WSCG, our local station, and now that she'd snagged Mac Tabor, the most eligible bachelor in Sugar Creek Gap, it was hard not to be envious of her.

Which made me wonder what Mac Tabor had seen in me. We dated for about a year before I had some sort of brain fart, thinking I wasn't in love with him after he asked me to marry him. Well, sort of. He'd sprung it on me like a big surprise. I didn't like surprises.

We were moving right along. Doing just fine as we enjoyed each other's company and wham! He wanted more. More than I could give.

I'd just moved into the new house I'd inherited from one of my mail route clients and gotten a new dog to add to my already ornery cat. I'd left the only house I'd ever known and loved by giving it to Grady and Julia so they could raise Clara and give me a whole bunch more grandbabies. That was stress.

Also, I'd found a couple of dead bodies in the past couple of years, and that didn't even add to the stress in my life. Sweet Clara's early arrival to the world was the biggest worry I had, so Mac had decided it was the perfect time to pile on me this whole notion of moving in and getting hitched when I was just fine with the companionship we'd been sharing.

To make matters even worse, Mac had been my deceased husband's best friend and around me all my life. Not that dating Mac made me worry about what Richard would've thought because, truth be told, Richard had cheated on me our entire marriage, which I didn't find out until ten years after he was killed in a car wreck, and this woman had shown up in Sugar Creek Gap.

Talk about a life changer.

Still.

Here I was, trying to hold a reverse warrior pose while Lucy Drake looked like a Zen queen.

Too bad she wasn't next to me, I might've lost my balance and knocked her over.

"You know you're not so subtle." Iris eyeballed me from underneath her long curly brown and somewhat gray hair.

"You look like you were in a windstorm." I couldn't help but point out how her fancy bun she'd so desperately tried to create on top of her head had fallen with each pose.

"Ha. Ha." She smiled and went back to reverse warrior.

"Back to warrior two." Peaches began to guide us back to standing, where we finally made it to the floor flat on our backs. "Close your eyes and place one hand on your heart while the other rests on your stomach."

Now, this was a pose I could get into.

"Inhale a long deep breath through the nose, then gently, in one long steady stream, release it out of the mouth while letting your eyes gently close." This was the part where Peaches walked around and placed a blanket over us. "Let your mind wander. Let your thoughts come and go without putting any sort of detail into them."

"Bernadette!"

I jerked up.

"What?" My eyes darted around the room.

"You fell asleep again." Iris nudged me with her big toe. "And you were snoring so loud."

"This class is killing me." I curled my legs up under me and let the blanket fall off of me. "Why didn't you just let me sleep? I swear I feel more rested now than I have all day."

"Ladies." Lucy Drake slinked over, the water bottle strap dangling from the crook of her finger. "Isn't this a fabulous class?" She bent over at her waist and touched her toes. "I've gotten so limber, and my muscles are hugging all my bones."

I hugged the blanket to me, trying to cover up the baggy sweatpants and old Sugar Creek Gap High School Grizzly Bear's sweatshirt that was Grady's when he was in high school.

"Off I go. My people have all their ears on what I've got to say in Coffee Chat. Hope you join." She wiggled her fingers and her fanny as she walked on by.

"I would ask what on earth Mac sees in her, but I won't. I can see it myself." Iris bent down and grabbed my yoga mat for me while I hobbled out of the big open room. "Did you hear me?"

"Of course, I heard you." I turned around and looked at the high wooden beamed ceiling and hardwood floors that created the echoing Zen den. "But so can everyone else."

I pointed my finger in the air when my voice echoed.

It was really a cool concept Peaches had when she'd bought the old building. It was a two-story mercantile store from when Sugar Creek Gap, Kentucky was a big mill town. We still had the very first working mill wheel at the very heart of downtown.

Like most towns, settlers had gone from land to land and built little communities along the way. Sugar Creek Gap had been built on generations of families. We were a small community, but through the years, the owners of big farms had sold off various acres and built several subdivisions along with big box stores on the outskirts of town.

But I worked, lived, and mainly stayed in downtown Sugar Creek Gap, leading me back to Tranquility Spa. Peaches wasn't going to be able to salvage the second floor of the building on the inside. She ended up gutting the entire inside where she had large wooden beams installed to create a very tall one-story shop. She was able to divide the large space into thirds. The larger room was her studio, another room had three separate massage beds along with appointments for her Reiki technique. Peaches had tried to get me in there.

No way, no how. When I Googled it, the information popped up that having such a massage performed on me might make my soul open up and I'd cry. I'd done enough crying for three lifetimes; I certainly didn't want to be a willing participant in anything that would make me cry.

The third section Peaches had built was the front reception where she conducted business transactions and had open wooden storage shelves for clients, along with some clothing racks where she sold yoga apparel.

"How much is this?" I asked Peaches when she walked past me.

"I don't know." China Gordon, Peaches best friend, smiled when she realized that I'd mistaken her for Peaches. "Peaches, price?" She lifted the Tranquility Spa water bottle up to her lips and took a drink, motioning me with the other hand to lift the pants in the air.

I held them up in the air and wondered if I needed to buy one of those bottles and just drink water all day long. Then maybe I'd look like them, as I recalled the one next to Lucy and always seeing Peaches with one.

"That's a wonderful fabric," Peaches called from the counter where she was sipping on some sort of green liquid. "You can always try it, and if you don't like it, you can get your money back."

Iris laughed.

"Are you seriously thinking about buying that?" she asked me as I held the very small pants. The entire thing was smaller than my one leg.

"Mmm." I shrugged. "Maybe." I gulped when I took a look at the price tag. "Do you think this is sixty dollars' worth of material?" I joked under my breath.

"I bet we can get Loetta Goldey to make us something for one-fourth of the price." Iris was serious.

"She knits." I let out a long sigh and looked at the yoga pants again.

"Or you can wait a few days and try the new line I'm representing," China said. "Right, Peaches?"

"We do need to have that meeting." Peaches flipped open the calendar on her desk, and China put her head down as they pointed to various dates.

China Gordon was a clothing representative for athletic wear. From all the times she'd stopped her mail, I knew she traveled a lot for work. No doubt she had to since Tranquility Spa would be the only place in Sugar Creek Gap she'd be able to get her athletic line to sell.

"I'd love to see the products you represent." I made the decision to buy the yoga pants and placed them on the counter.

"Oh no, Bernie. China has finally decided to take my advice and come up with her own line to sell." Peaches had so much pride on her face for her best friend. She rang up my pants and took my debit card from me. "Since she is almost finished getting her 300 hours of yoga training, so she can teach some classes, she knows the right fabrics that'll help your body move and stretch to its fullest potential."

"Congratulations, China. That's wonderful news." I loved to see young people go for their dreams. "I'll be the first customer."

"And that's why we need to get our little meeting on the books," China told Peaches.

"We will." Peaches held a finger up in the air to answer the ringing phone.

"I'll see you Wednesday," I mouthed and took the bag from Peaches so she didn't have to stop her phone conversation.

"No. I'm the owner. I do not have to let her take yoga classes." Peaches didn't sound so happy with the person on the other end of the line. I couldn't help but listen in while I waited on Iris to get her shoes on. "If she comes in here, she'll regret it. And for that matter, don't you ever step foot in here either."

Iris couldn't stop herself from lingering. Her big ears and eyes were taking it all in, and Peaches knew it. Peaches slowly turned around and covered the phone with her hand as she continued to whisper with a very angry tone.

I tugged on Iris's sweatshirt and nodded toward the door.

"Wonder what that was about?" Iris asked once we made it outside where the sun was still out before dusk, which made me so happy. I could take little Clara outside when I went to visit them tonight. "Or who it was about?"

"Who knows. Somebody always has a beef with someone around here." I sighed, knowing Peaches Partin was one of the gentlest of souls. When you were around her, she radiated calm, and I swear there was a light that came right out of her soul and spread across the world through her eyes. "I'll walk you to your car."

Since I lived a street behind Main Street on Little Creek Road, I practically walked everywhere. According to Doctor Hunter, walking just wasn't enough for a middle-aged woman like myself. When did I become middle-aged? I still thought of my mother as middle-aged, not me.

Iris stopped dead in her tracks while I was deep in thought, knocking right into her.

"I don't have a good feeling." Iris had this funny look on her face. Her face clouded over like a thundercloud, making me get chilled to the bone.

CHAPTER 2

Iris and I didn't talk about her feeling. She got these about every three-to-six months, to which nothing good ever came out of them. Though her feelings weren't always spot on, they were pretty close not to take note and keep an eye out.

Instead of trying to figure out what she'd felt, I walked her to her car and safely put her in, telling her to call me if she needed me. Something I might regret, but hey, I wasn't sleeping well anyway.

Buster and Rowena were happy to see me when I walked in the door of my little house. Buster wiggled and jiggled all over, satisfied with a few kisses and pats before he darted to the front door to go outside.

Rowena dragged her long orange tail around my chin, purring loudly and putting a smile on my face.

"I missed you too." I scooped her up into my arms and walked back with her into the kitchen to get her a salmon treat, which happened to be her second favorite. Chicken was her first, but I was out and knew she had her regular veterinary checkup for the year, so salmon was going to have to do until the vet visit.

Rowena meowed and rubbed against my ankles as though she were trying to hurry me up. Once I'd put the treats on the ground, she ignored me, daintily eating them.

"You be good while me and Buster head out to the farmhouse to see Clara," I told Rowena on my way down the hallway to our bedroom, peeling off the sweatpants. I took the yoga pants out of the Tranquility Wellness bag and decided to pour myself into them.

Pour was about right.

"Oh, dear gawd," I groaned when I turned to look at myself. Even Rowena came in to see what I was up to. "Two things that tell the truth, Rowena," I said, taking another look at my butt, "children and yoga pants."

Quickly, I took them off and threw them back into the bag before tossing them into the back of my closet. Out of sight, out of mind.

The slightest things really did make a mood sour, so instead of dwelling on it, I put my sweatpants back on. Clara didn't care what her granny wore.

"Now, you be good," I told Rowena and grabbed the keys to my car along with the box of food my mom gave me to take over to Julia when I delivered the mail to the Wallflower Diner, our family-owned restaurant on Main Street.

Rowena, satisfied, really couldn't give two cents what I did now since she'd gotten her treats. She had her leg straight up in the air and licked all her leg, down to her toenails.

"Are you trying to give me some sort of subliminal message about how good and limber you are, or how much better at yoga you are than me?" I questioned her with a side-eye.

Of course, she responded by rolling over onto her back and contorting into a position that would require me to see an emergency chiropractor.

With the door locked behind me and an excited Buster trotting along next to me, we got into my car and rolled out of downtown into the country where the old family farm was located.

Buster kept his head out the window the entire time. He seemed steady enough, but I still put a hand on him for safekeeping.

The farmhouse and farm had been passed down to me from my parents after I'd gotten pregnant with Grady. Recently, I'd done the same after I found out Julia was pregnant with little Clara.

They'd lived over the family diner in the small one-bedroom apartment until they'd moved out here.

With each new day, Julia had been doing some major renovations, thanks to Mac Tabor. He was a brilliant architect and loved Grady and Julia like his own. That's what made our breakup so hard, but it would be fine. That's what I told myself.

The long gravel driveway was long gone now that they'd moved in. It was one of the first things to go because Grady didn't want Clara playing in gravel in fear she'd skin her knee.

I agreed. I'd only had Grady, and I didn't mind him skinning his knee. After all, he was rough and tumble. Gravel or no gravel, Grady always had some sort of cut.

Not for my sweet Clara.

The tires hummed over the old cattle grate that was still at the entrance of the farm, which brought back a lot of memories of my childhood when my daddy had many cows and the grate was supposed to keep them in the property. One or two got out on occasion, but for the most part, it did its job of keeping them in.

The excitement bubbled up in me the closer I got to the farmhouse, only to be busted as soon as I saw Mac's truck there.

I sucked in a deep breath and thought about the images Peaches Partin put in our heads at the end of yoga class that made me take a little catnap. Unfortunately, I realized I'd fallen asleep every single time she started to give us an image to focus on.

I sucked in another deep breath and opened the door. Buster darted over me and bolted out the door, leaving me to fend for myself alone. But I was armed with a gift for Clara and food for them. Something Mac would never do.

But dang it if it wasn't something Lucy Drake would do.

I nearly had a full-blown anxiety attack when I looked in the screen door of the house and saw my grandbaby in Lucy Drake's arms, with Mac smiling and goggling over Lucy's shoulder.

My heart started to palpitate. My breath quickened. My mind raced with fear of how much Clara appeared to be enjoying them, wondering if I was going to be good enough. Pretty enough. Small enough. My gut wrenched, and I thought I was going to be sick right there on their front porch. My front porch. My family front porch. Grady's front porch.

My palms began to sweat, and I could feel myself making an exit plan. A quick getaway, which I'd become very good at over the past few months since Mac and I had called it quits.

Leave it to Buster to bark, making everyone look at me. I could see it now. Mac's thoughts as his eyes darted back and forth between me and Lucy.

Wow. Look at Lucy compared to Bernie. What was I thinking? Lucy's hair is so long and pretty. She looks great in these yoga pants (which she was still in). *Poor Bernie. She's completely let herself go in those sweatpants* (I'm sure Lucy told him she'd seen me and how I was snoring). *Glad I got out when I did.*

"Bernie!" Mac finally took the initiative to break the most disturbing and very uncomfortable silence. "There's the maw-maw."

Maw-maw? Like hee-haw or something so hillbilly like that? No, thank you.

"I don't..." I started to protest.

"Mom, Julia and I've been teaching Clara to call you Mawmaw and showing her the cute photo album you gave her." Grady seemed awfully pleased with the name.

He opened the screen door.

"Who came up with..." I was about to protest again when Lucy Drake opened her big mouth.

"You're the perfect maw-maw," she giggled. "Look, you're already bringing food." She lifted her thin fingers to her tiny little skintight yoga shirt, placing a flat palm on her chest. "I had a maw-maw, and she did the same thing. But I have to tell you it wasn't good for her hips or mine." She winked then looked at little Clara. "Isn't that right, sweet Clara?" Lucy spoke baby talk to my baby, causing me to hard swallow the bitter words I so desperately wanted to spit into her perfectly made-up face. I was only worried it would affect my Clara.

The more she bounced Clara on her skinny hip bone, the more Clara giggled and smiled right back at her.

"Mom, you okay?" Grady took me by the arm.

"I'm fine." I handed him the box. "This is from your grandmother."

"Grandmother?" Grady laughed at my formality because we didn't call her that at all. He leaned in like he was giving me a kiss but whispered in my ear, "Are you okay with this?"

I grabbed his hand and squeezed it with a big smile on my face.

"Let Maw-maw see her little Clara." I marched over in my oversized sweatpants and sweatshirt, plucking Clara right out of Lucy's arms.

"Thank you for the food." Julia got up from the chair and came over to hug me. "I'm starving."

I followed her into the kitchen where they'd recently torn down a lot of the old farmhouse walls to make their living space and kitchen open concept.

"I'm sorry. I had no idea Mac was bringing her." Julia's brows furrowed, and she gave me and Clara another big hug.

"No problem," I said in a happy voice with a big smile on my face and looked at those sweet little cupid bow lips Clara had. Her skin was perfect, and she had the bluest of eyes. "I've got to get used to it."

"Maybe you need to explore why it bothers you." Julia opened the cabinets and took out a couple of plates. "Is it possible you do want to spend your life with him?"

"Ahhh, we don't need to talk about boys, do we?" I asked Clara, and she smiled so big.

"What are y'all talking about in here?" Lucy Drake made an appearance. "The boys are talking remodel, and I don't get into those things."

"I was just getting me and Grady a plate of food." Julia reached in to get a third dish. "Would you like some? Plenty for everyone."

The food did look good, and I was about to say I'd take a couple of scoops, but then...

"No." Lucy waved her off. "I just got out of yoga, and I can never eat after a soul workout." She turned her attention to me. "Right, Bernie?"

"Yeah. None for me." It was hard to say through a mouthful of water. "I'm definitely not hungry." I tried to cover up the loud growl coming from my gut and not notice Julia looking at my stomach.

"Ohh." Lucy wiggled her shoulders. "You're getting a great gut workout if your stomach is gurgling and you're not hungry."

"Yeah." I shrugged and sat down with Clara in my arms. "Julia, she's perfect." I decided to focus on what was right with the world, and it was right in my arms.

"She's pretty great. And her Uncle Mac is just so excited about her." I could feel Lucy standing over me. "I hope you don't mind I came with him. I was at yoga, with Bernie"—she said it like it made it better—"and I just popped over to Mac's house. Unannounced, of course, when I found him getting into his truck." She snorted and sat down in the chair next to me. "When he told me he was coming here, I sorta invited myself."

"You know how it is around Sugar Creek Gap." Julia put both plates on the family farmhouse table where we'd gathered every single Sunday since I was born and to this day to have our weekly family supper.

That included Mac too. He still came every Sunday, but if he started to bring Lucy, I'd have to put a halt to him coming. That was that.

Julia continued, "You can just stop by without calling or anything. Our door is always open."

I scowled. That was one invitation Lucy Drake would burn in her perfect-sized brain. In fact, I stared at her brain and wondered if she had any gray matter like I did. Or that's what Dr. Hunter told me I had.

"See those little white specs?" Dr. Hunter had asked me at my annual checkup, where she did a full-body midlife checkup along with a full blood panel just to make sure I was aging alright. "You don't need to worry about those. That's just aging brain."

That certainly didn't make me feel good. That was also the same visit where she'd told me I needed to do better exercise for my bones and how yoga and Lucy Drake entered my weekly routine.

Yeah. I saw Lucy Drake when I delivered the radio station mail, but I did everything in my power to deliver it when she was on air and not somewhere she'd see me.

So, whenever I was at the Wallflower Diner, just a few doors down from WSCG, and Lucy came on after a song, I'd hightail it down there to deliver the mail. No different than thinking I could avoid Mac and his architecture firm and house by delivering in the afternoon.

Julia was right about one thing. Maybe I did need to explore why this little situation with Lucy and Mac bothered me so much.

But not tonight. Tonight, I was going to visit with my little Clara.

"Who is Maw-maw's girl?" I asked Clara in a baby voice as I snuggled her closer.

If I was going to be a maw-maw, I was going to be the best damn maw-maw in the south. You could bet your grits on that.

CHAPTER 3

Iris was laughing so hard through the phone after I told her about Lucy Drake telling me how my gut health was awesome due to the yoga I'd done before going to see Clara, that I had to take the phone from my ear in fear I'd lose my hearing.

Right now, that was about the only body part working.

"That is the funniest thing." Iris couldn't stop herself. "I bet you were about to kill that woman."

"That's really not the worst part." I buttoned up my blue mail carrier shirt and headed down to the kitchen where my morning brewed coffee was a welcoming smell. "Grady insists Clara calls' me Maw-maw."

Just saying the words nearly made me gag.

"For heaven's sake!" Iris squealed in delight. "Stop making me laugh. My stomach is killing me from yoga."

While she continued to hoot and carry on, I did my morning ritual with the fur babies before filling up a to-go mug and heading out the door into the dark morning.

"You might have to have a talk with Grady about making sure he texts you when Mac is over." Iris made a good point. "But

Julia is right. You do need to explore why it bothers you so much since you're the one who called it off between you two."

I changed the subject. "Are you at the bakery?" I'd spent all night thinking about this, and I didn't want my first thoughts of the day to be about it, especially when I'd not gotten any sort of divine intervention on why I did feel the way I felt.

Trust me when I said that I'd prayed, screamed, and cried all night long to find some sort of peace in the matter.

"I am. A full day ahead of deliveries. So many birthdays in the summer, which goes to show just what couples do when they are cooped up in the winter." Iris always had a funny way of looking at things. "If I'm not there when you deliver my mail, make sure you get the outgoing bills from Geraldine."

Geraldine Workman was an employee of Iris's and mainly worked the counter.

"I will." I hung up, quickly crossed over Main Street, and walked behind the post office where the employee entrance and the slew of LLV (short for lifelong vehicles) were. "Hey there, Nick Kirby. What a bright way to start my day."

Nick had been one of Grady's high school friends. Instead of going off to college, he got his mechanics certificate. That kid could fix anything. He was as handy as a pocket on a shirt when it came to farm equipment breaking down.

If I fed him a good meal, he'd fix just about anything.

Now that he's grown up, like all these boys seemed to have done, he co-owned the local mechanics shop where he rented garage space just a couple of blocks from downtown, which just so happened to be on the border of my third loop, making them not on my route.

"Mrs. Butler." He went to hug me but pulled back. He showed me his hands. "I'm all dirty, and you look so clean in your mail outfit."

"Are you kidding me?" I put my arms out. "I don't care, and I could use a hug this morning."

Nick smiled and wrapped me up in a big grizzly bear hug like he did when he was a kid.

"How's your mama and them? I've not seen them in a long time, now that you kids are all grown up." I looked up at him. Another thing. These little boys had all grown taller than me too.

"They are good. In fact, my mom bought Clara a present and said she was going to drop it off once Julia got back on her feet." He smiled, and the dimples in his cheeks deepened. He shook his head, pulling the towel out from the mechanic's overalls to wipe his hands. "I still can't believe Grady Butler is a dad."

"He did good, kiddo." I had that stupid happy grin on my face that I'd seen so many other grandmothers have. "How 'bout you? You seeing anyone?"

"Nah." By the way he said it, I could tell he was lying. "No one serious. Not yet. But when I do, I'll let you know. But that means you have to stop by the garage more than once a month."

"Now that I live in town, I walk everywhere and these"—I looked down and wiggled my feet—"do not require gas or service."

Service was a stretch, but he didn't need to know how they ached.

"You were always so fun. Clara is going to be one lucky grandkid." He pointed to the old mail trucks. "The government isn't paying me to stand around and gab this early. I've got to get some of these vehicles running."

"Yep." I looked at the old things. "The government won't replace them. That's why they're called lifelong vehicles." I nodded and waved him off. "Tell your parents to stop by and see me."

"Mama would love that. Have a good day. It's supposed to be gorgeous." He plunged back into the guts of one of the little cars as I headed inside to get my first loop of mail.

The Sugar Creek Gap Nursing Home and Senior Living Facility.

The facility was located behind the post office which made it super easy as my first loop of the day. After I filled the residents' mailboxes there, I would stop back by the post office to grab the mail for my second loop, which included all the downtown shops and my street of a few houses.

Today, the nursing home went by much quicker than usual. My dear friend who was always waiting on me, Vince Caldwell, had taken a month-long vacation to visit his son out west. Vince wasn't in the care facility department; he was in the condos located on the property. In fact, my parents had moved out there after they were built.

It was perfect for independent living, and there was very little yard to maintain, though my mom about threw a duck fit when the community didn't allow her to plant whatever flowers she wanted in the front yard, even though her backyard was a flowering oasis.

Filling the communal mailboxes was easy and I was on my way in no time. Especially since no one was even awake at this hour.

Plus, without the distraction, I would get my mail route delivered earlier so I could meet Julia at the doctor's office to babysit Clara while she went in for her health check. This was going to be a big one too. The doctor was supposed to clear her to go back to work. I couldn't help but worry what that meant for Clara. I'd tried six ways from Sunday to work my finances so I could retire and keep her myself when Julia went back to work. But Richard didn't leave me in any shape financially, and I'd given the only real thing I owned to Grady, which was the farm. And I'd not been at the post office long enough to draw any sort of good retirement, so my worries would have to stay until Julia figured out what she was going to do.

The thought of that precious baby getting her hair pulled by some mean child or even the thought of one of them giving her a running nose just hurt me to my core.

I shook it off and grabbed the next loop of mail, sticking it into my mail carrier bag and off I went on the rest of my morning route. The downtown businesses were on the left side of Main Street as I walked toward Short Street. The old mill was located at the far end across from Short Street, which still had a flowing creek that ran along the right side of the street, making the area a historic sight and unavailable for anyone to build on. But on the other side of the old mill wheel was the courthouse, fire and sheriff's department, as well as the town's library and funeral home. After those shops' mail were delivered, I would head down Short Street to Little Creek Road, where I'd deliver my neighbor's mail.

I always gave a little extra time for my street because I knew the Front Porch Ladies—the few houses between my house and Mac Tabor's house, where the widows of the community loved to gather on each other's porches, or even just holler between porches. But they always loved to chitchat and try to quiz me on various pieces of mail others had gotten. Plus, they were big in the Publishers Clearing House Sweepstakes, and they knew exactly what time of the month their manila envelope came.

Bless their hearts, I'd tried to tell them a million times how half the other residents of Sugar Creek Gap were also holding their breaths for the sweepstakes van, balloons, flowers, and the big check to show up at their house, and how they were wasting their money on the various magazine subscriptions and whatever else they had to buy in order to enter, as well.

They'd roll their eyes and believed one of them was gonna be the big winner. I'd learned to keep my mouth shut.

After I finished my second loop, I'd sometimes grab Buster and take him on my third loop, which was my biggest. There was a large neighborhood that was located behind the old mill wheel and the courthouse. It was one of those neighborhoods where there was one house after the other. Not cheap houses either. It was a sought-out neighborhood because it was convenient to downtown and the high school, not to mention the fancy country club attached to the subdivision.

There were so many dirty little secrets back there that I felt like I was walking into a soap opera on my third loop. People didn't realize just how much your mail carrier can tell about you by delivering your mail.

Since the subdivision was right behind the post office as well, it was easiest to make it my final destination, drop off any mail that wasn't able to be delivered at the post office, cross Main Street, slip over one of the few bridges that connected Little Creek Road to Main Street, and I was home.

Briefly, I stopped to listen to the sound of the babbling brook swimming across the rocks as the old mill pushed the water down the creek. It was a daily ritual that I loved. I think it was more soothing to my aching muscles than the yoga class. I hoisted my bag up on my shoulder and crossed the street.

Social Knitwork was my first stop. It was easy to simply head into the yarn shop, drop any mail in the basket Loetta Goldey left on the counter, and grab anything she had stamped. Most of the time, I delivered the mail around the same time, and she was always teaching some sort of craft class.

Once I'd gotten the big idea from the Front Porch Ladies to take a knitting class. It turned out that I should never listen to the Front Porch Ladies.

The next stop was Tranquility Wellness. I knew I didn't have to worry about seeing Peaches because she had a standing hot yoga class every day at this time. Thank goodness my class was every other night because I'm sure I'd not be walking if it was daily.

Peaches Partin was a brilliant business owner. She knew when she opened the spa that her clients wanted to feel pampered and relaxed. There was a correlation between the brain and the smell, or so she claimed after I'd once asked her about the amazing smell that not only filled her shop but flowed outside, spilling into the open air.

"You smell that?" she had asked me with big bright eyes the first day she'd opened. "That's a big smiley." I could recall how her mouth spread across her face in a huge smile. But it was the big deep breath she had me take that made me feel so calm. "That." She'd pointed her finger at me. "That calm feeling is because of the fresh tropical, lavender scent I purposely have pumped through the ventilation that makes you all calm and relaxed."

I'll never forget how amazed I was that you could pump any smell you wanted through a ventilation.

I loved delivering the mail. I had my routine with every shop. Tranquility Wellness was one of my favorites since no one was in the reception area. I was able to step inside, take a few deep cleansing breaths of that fabulous smell, and it was like a reset to my brain.

Just like every morning, I took a big deep breath, curled my hand around the handle, and opened the door, ready to finish off the inhale with a nose full of calm.

"I'm telling you to get out!" Peaches's long red braid was pulled around her shoulder and dangled down past her chest. The light-blue one-piece yoga outfit had a shimmery sheen to it. "I'll call the sheriff," she warned the similarly built brunette.

"You can't just kick out a customer. I've paid up a full year." The young woman was standing her ground. "I'm going in there to do hot yoga, so call the sheriff." Her voice was much calmer than Peaches.

"Over my dead body or yours." Peaches slid her body between the door of the studio and the other woman.

"Ladies"—the voice of reason came from China Gordon—"this is ridiculous. We are all women of light and love. We want nothing but the best for all of us." She had a pashmina shawl in her hands and put it in the young woman's hands. "Sarah, this is from my new line. Why don't you go and enjoy this today?"

"It still doesn't get me my hot yoga class or my money. I've got a good six months left on my membership." Sarah rested her hands on her hips, shifting her small frame side to side.

"You want your money back?" Peaches was acting so out of character; her actions made my insides tense up. She caught my eye when she marched to the counter and poked her finger on the fancy electronic tablet, making a drawer pop open underneath the counter. She grabbed a fistful of money and stalked right back to Sarah, throwing what looked to be all one-hundred-dollar bills into her face.

My jaw dropped watching all those Benjamins fall to the floor.

"You'll regret this," Sarah said with a smack of bitterness in her voice. She reached down and picked up the money. "Simon always said you were a big pill to swallow, and this little Zen den of yours was all an act. He mentioned how you are one of the worst gossips in Sugar Creek Gap, but I refused to believe it. You seemed so nice, and well"—Sarah's eyes drew up and down Peaches—"let's just say it appears you walk your talk of love, happiness, kindness." Sarah held the money in one fist and shook it in the air. "But you're all talk. You disgust me, and I'll tell everyone I know."

"Good! Get out!" Peaches screamed when Sarah walked past

the counter to go out the door. I took a step aside so I wasn't in the way.

"Forget her." China was trying to be a good friend and calm Peaches down. "Let's take a look at these samples. You're going to love them."

"Not now, China." Peaches pushed her hand aside. "I have to go meditate and get Simon and that... that..." She stormed back to one of the massage rooms.

I carefully laid the mail on the counter and went to turn around, but China started talking to me.

"I'm not sure if Peaches will ever be right, now that she and Simon have broken up." China shook her head and placed her garments back in the bag. "That was his new girlfriend. She never took a yoga class before Simon. Now she's signed up for all sorts of classes, and I bet it's just to get Peaches's goat."

"That's a shame because I saw the same girl in here the other day, and they were having words then." I couldn't help but notice China's shirt looked like a yoga shirt but a little looser fitting around the bottom. "I guess I can relate to Peaches."

"You should tell her that." China shrugged.

"Can I ask where you got your shirt?" I couldn't take my eyes off of it.

"It's one of mine. It's a tented bottom so it flows when your moving from position to position." She held her arms out to the side.

"I love it. Will Peaches be selling it here?" It was definitely something I could wear and feel some confidence in until I got the Lucy Drake body.

"That's why I'm here this morning. We are trying to go over some final choices, but poor Peaches just isn't in the right frame of mind to even think about any big business decisions." She sat down on the stool behind the counter.

"Are you working here?" I asked when I noticed her getting comfortable.

"Oh no. I have to head out of town this afternoon for my real sales job, but I figured I can wait a few more minutes until Peaches comes back." China placed the palms of her hands together and bent her head down. "Some good meditation will make her feel a million times better."

"If you do get that top in the shop, please hold one for me. I'd buy it today."

"I can probably fit you for one at my house and make you one, if you want." She took something from her bag of clothes, and leaning on the counter with her elbows propping her up, she held a small business card between her fingers. "Give me a call."

"Really?" I was so pleased. "That would be great. I'm just not so comfortable wearing all the tighter-fitting clothes just yet."

"Then you are the perfect customer for my line." She sat back and crossed her arms. "I keep telling Peaches that the older woman is who will love my line of clothing."

"Thanks." I snickered with her card in my grip and headed out the door. "Older woman," I groaned, rolling my eyes and heading into the next shop, the Wallflower Diner.

I about knocked over one of the customers walking out of the Wallflower because my mind was all knotted up in trying to figure out what on earth about me said "older woman".

"Older woman?" My mom cackled from behind the counter. She shoved a piece of Kentucky Hot Brown breakfast casserole in my face along with a hot cup of coffee. "Honey, you take a good gander at this face. I'm the older woman."

"You're a youngin'." My dad scooted down to the open stool next to me. "You'll always be my baby."

"I bet the jumbled mess in your head is all about the change." Mom pointed a direct finger at me. She grabbed the coffeepot and made her way down the counter, topping off the customers' coffee cups.

"Oh dear." Dad took off his John Deere cap and rubbed his hand over what was left of his gray hair. "Your mom was a doozy to deal with when she was going through the change."

I smiled.

"Lucky for her she had you." I took one more look at the fattening casserole and decided my diet wasn't such a good thing either.

"Why you eyeballing my food?" Mom took great offense to anyone who ordered from the diner and didn't devour it as soon as she set it down. "What's wrong with you?"

"The change," Dad snarled and brought his coffee up to his lips, taking a drink.

"Oh honey, you need to go see Doc Faith. She'll give you something because if you don't get a handle on it now, you're gonna be having your own personal summer in there." She circled her finger in front of me. "Now"—she pushed the plate closer—"eat up."

"I'll take it to go." I looked at my watch so she'd think I was telling the truth. "I'm running late." I bent down and picked out their mail, which also included their personal mail.

Truth be told, I'd never want to hurt my mom's feelings, and her food was delicious. That was the problem. I'd seen all those pop-up ads on Facebook, and the internet talked all about the change.

I swear, sometimes I felt there was a little bug in my computer that could read my mind. Anytime I even thought about something, the next thing I knew, that thing I was thinking of or even mentioned had some sort of ad pop up on my devices.

Mom leaned over, nearly knocking my coffee into my lap, and slapped her hand across my forehead.

"Nope. No fever." She pulled back. "Listen, you might have something else if you ain't hungry. I saw on Oprah how this lady thought she was going through the change." Mom's eyes drew up and down my body. "She lost her appetite too. It was awful. I'll spare you the details until you see Faith."

"Mom, Oprah isn't on anymore." I stood up and watched her grab a to-go box and push the casserole into it.

"I know that. I saw it once." She reached under the counter and put another to-go box on top of my other to-go box. "You don't forget things you see on Oprah."

"Then it all must be true," my dad groaned and rolled his eyes, taking the mail from me.

I tried not to laugh out loud, but Mom saw it anyway.

"That there," she said, tapping the top box, "is some freshly baked smoky summer sausage and grits casserole for Millie Barnes. She's entertaining some of the Elk's women this afternoon, and I told her I'd send some slices with you."

"No problem." Then I watched her stack another box on top of the other two.

"That is for my grand-fur-babies."

Every time, without fail, I left the diner with something equally delicious for Rowena and Buster.

"Now, do you want me to send something to Mac?" Her chin slid slightly to the side, the opposite direction of her eyes as they bore into my soul. She tapped her fingernail to her chest. "Way to a man's heart is the stomach, right, honey?"

"Mmhhmmm." Dad was too busy separating his mail into categories, which I've never understood. He held out a piece of mail. "This ain't ours."

"Oh." I took it and noticed it was a certified letter that needed a signature. "Monica is generally really good about separating out any sort of special deliveries," I said, talking about the mail clerk who took pride in separating out the mail before anyone even got to work. "Simon Little?"

That was super strange. Simon Little was Nick Kirby's business partner at the garage who just so happened to be Peaches Partin's ex and Sarah Hodge's new boyfriend. Boy, things were coming around full circle.

"When did you start delivering to the gas station?" Dad had already seen who it belonged to.

"I don't, but that means I have to get going so I can take the extra walk there to get it where it needs to go." It was a perfect time to get out of there because my stomach was really growling. If Mom heard that, she'd lay herself in front of the diner door until I ate the entire contents of my to-go box. Plus, it let me off the hook from answering any questions about Mac Tabor.

"You give me some sugar." Mom held her arms out and walked around the corner, giving me a peck on the cheek. She patted her hands on my back. "You let me know what Faith says."

If my mom was one thing, she was persistent. I'd never even committed to going to see Doctor Faith Hunter, but in Mom's mind, her even suggesting it meant that I already had an appointment.

I waved goodbye to them and quickly delivered the mail to Pie in the Face, where I grabbed the outgoing mail from Geraldine Workman like Iris had told me to. Then I dropped off the mail to the Community Center and the Roasted Bean coffee shop before I found myself standing face-to-face with Mac Tabor in his office.

"Thanks." He greeted me with his big white smile, taking me back to the first time I'd met him when Richard and I were dating. At the time, I'd felt horrible and guilty about my thoughts about Mac.

Why wasn't I dating him, I remember thinking to myself

when I'd gotten swept up into his deep brown eyes and thoughts of me running my hands through his thick brown hair—compared to Richard's thin short hair.

But that was years ago, and here we stood today. He still had those amazing deep eyes and thick brown hair, with only a few wrinkles.

"What's with the look?" Mac asked. None of my expressions ever went unnoticed by him.

"You could always tell when I was thinking something." I smiled and handed him his mail. "I was just thinking how unfair it is how a man can get better looking with time while we women start falling apart."

"Oh. This sounds like something you need to discuss with Iris." He wasn't going to touch that with a ten-foot pole.

I laughed.

"That is every woman but your woman." My jaw dropped when I blurted out the words without any sort of filter. My mind didn't even process it before I said it. "I'm so sorry. Lucy is a beautiful woman. I—"

"You forget that I know you better than probably anyone, and I'm already used to you just saying stuff." He put a comforting hand on my arm, which sent electric shocks through me, causing me to take a step back. "Sorry. I really shouldn't think I can touch you like that anymore."

"It's fine. I've got to get going." I gestured to the door.

"Is this how it's going to be now that we aren't..." He stumbled for the right words.

"Going to get married? Hitched? Live together?" There I went again, blurting stuff out.

Maybe there was something to this middle-aged woman thing that went along with saying whatever I felt like.

I gulped.

"I'm so sorry. I am losing my mind." I shook my head. "I'm

happy for you and Lucy. I don't know what this is for me, but you'll be the first to know." I didn't wait around for him to have a comeback before I hightailed it out of there.

Lucky for me, after I'd delivered the mail to the General Store, Lucy was on the radio, so I was able to slip into the station lobby without her seeing me. Then I went across the street where I delivered the mail to the courthouse, fire and sheriff's departments, as well as the library and funeral home.

What made my second loop so easy to do was the perfect timing. It was right when things were just getting going for the day, making all the shop owners and various employees too busy to gab and slow me down.

And today they all seemed busy, which put me ahead of schedule. So I could take a little longer walk to the gas station to deliver Simon's certified letter to him before I went back to Little Creek Road, where I was sure Millie Barnes was waiting for me to deliver the to-go box from the Wallflower Mom had sent with me.

Even with the food deep in my mail carrier bag, my stomach growled as the smell of freshly homemade food wafted out and up to my nose.

"Resist the urge," I told myself and continued to walk a little faster when I noticed the old Phillips 66 gas sign in front of me.

The old gas station was the first one that was ever put in Sugar Creek Gap. Now there were many more throughout the town, but this one in particular was like you were stepping back in time.

They had two pumps, one on each side of the other, a small office with a few vending machines, a restroom around the side, and a large glass garage door. Nick Kirby and Simon Little rented the garage from the owners to do all their mechanic work.

Not only did I love how Colvin Batty had rented the extra

space to Nick and Simon, since he was too old to do any work, but it was a nice way to keep the gas station open for business. So many businesses had closed after all the big retail stores and fancy gas stations were built on the outskirts of the city limits.

Still, Nick and Simon not only benefited, but so did Colvin. He was a resident of the Sugar Creek Gap Nursing Home, assisted living care, and the seven-thousand-a-month price tag to live there wasn't cheap.

I particularly loved the fact the gas attendant, a young high school boy, pumped your gas and washed your windshield just like they did when I was a kid. It was good ole Southern hospitality.

"Hey, Bernie." Nick pushed himself out from underneath the hood of a car. He took the rag dangling off the car he was working on and wiped the grease from his hands. The radio blurred music from WSCG. "Is Gerome alright?" He reached over to the old transistor and turned the volume knob down.

"Aww, he's fine. He'll probably be by shortly, but I noticed there's a certified letter that must've been accidentally put in my bag by mistake." I took my bag off my shoulder and reached into the front pocket where I'd put the letter so I didn't have to dig through the rest of the mail. "Is Simon here?"

Nick eyeballed the envelope.

"No, he went to see Tim Crouse about a part we've been trying to get manufactured for motorcycles." He reached out for the envelope. "I'll sign."

"I'm sorry. Only he can sign for it, but it is from the United States Patent and Trademark Office." I held the front of the letter out. "Maybe it's about your part. That's exciting."

His eyes zeroed in on the letter, and confusion settled in them.

"Nah. It must be something else because he said he filed the paperwork online under both of our names." He crossed his arms and appeared to be considering the situation.

"If I hustle back, I just might be able to catch him at the courthouse." I'd already been there to deliver the mail to those offices before I walked here, and I did have to pass it on my way back so I could get the mail to Little Creek Road delivered before the Front Porch Ladies had a hissy fit. "I better be on my way. It was good to see you, and good luck on your patent. You two are going to be famous!"

CHAPTER 4

There was no luck when I made it back to the courthouse and up the stairs to Tim Crouse's office. "I can give it to him." Tim Crouse reached for it when I showed it to him. "I'll be meeting with him again tomorrow to finalize some paperwork for it."

"I appreciate it, but even though you're his lawyer, I'm not able to leave it with you, by law." I shrugged and stuck it back in the front of the mailbag. "But let him know that I'll take it back to the post office tomorrow morning and have Gerome bring it to the gas station tomorrow."

"I'll do that," Tim agreed. "Say, I hated to hear about you and Mac."

"Yeah. You know, it was a bit uncomfortable with him being Richard's best friend, and honestly, I'm not really looking for a commitment." I slapped my flapping lips together when I realized what I'd said.

"You okay? You look a little shocked." Tim smiled and eased back onto the secretary's desk, who wasn't in the reception area, thank goodness.

"I guess I have no idea why I would even tell you that. I'm so sorry." I blinked my eyes, trying to blink some sense back into me.

"I guess being your lawyer, maybe you trust me with some deep dark secrets," he teased, though he was right.

Tim was someone I did trust. He'd really helped me out with all my legal dealings and the mess Richard had created with his other life. But that was in the past, and those were feelings I'd already decided to bury and not bring up anymore.

"I guess." I offered a reassuring smile, knowing he'd keep what I said between us. "Strange. Anyways, he and Lucy look very happy." That entire sentence was like I'd just swallowed a bitter pill, almost making me gag.

But like the true Southern lady I was, at least when I had on the mail carrier uniform, I was trying to stay positive and happy.

"You know I'm always here if you need an ear." Tim pushed off the desk and looked over my shoulder. His secretary had come in and handed him some papers.

"Hey, Bernie." Deborah pushed her glasses up her nose. "Did you forget to drop off a piece of mail?"

"Nope. Just trying to catch Simon Little."

"It was good to see you twice in a day." She smiled and walked behind her desk to answer the phone. "Line one." She looked at Tim.

"I'll talk to you later, Bernie."

"See ya, Tim." I waved bye to him and Deborah.

Of course, Tim had to mention Mac, but I had to mention Lucy. I knew she and Tim had gone on a few dates, which made me wonder if he needed to talk about Mac and Lucy more than me. There were plenty of times I'd see Tim around town and wonder how he was doing with it, though I didn't recall he and Lucy being what I'd consider officially a couple.

Quack, quack.

My duck friend who lived in the Little Creek was waiting for me at the small walking bridge over the creek on Short Street. It was a daily ritual. She'd wait for me near the bridge, and I'd throw her some duck pellet food I'd gotten from Veterinarian Olson. It was a nice place to stop and rest for a few minutes before I finished the second loop of deliveries.

"I'm sorry I'm late." I grabbed the bag of pellets from the mailbag and opened it up, tossing a handful into the creek. "I had to make a pit stop."

I had no idea why I talked to my duck friend, but I did. We would do the same song and dance at the end of Little Creek Road, where I'd cross over the other bridge at the end of the street that led me back to Main Street and across the street to the post office, where I'd grab my third and final loop of the day.

Quack, quack. The little duck looked so peaceful sitting on top of the water, only I knew its little webbed feet were going a mile a minute underneath the water to keep it from drowning.

"I feel like I'm drowning," I told the duck and threw one small handful of food into the creek. "I guess I'm wondering if I'm going to be alone when I'm older. How is this going to turn out for me?" I questioned the duck, who was safe to talk to since she didn't answer me back.

Her head pierced the water as her bill batted at the pellets, giving a little headshake a few times. I watched in amazement at how determined she was to eat every little pellet.

"I'll see you in a few minutes." I pushed the strap of the bag onto my shoulder, and off I went, taking a left on Little Creek Road.

There were only a few houses to deliver to on my street. First one was Mac Tabor. I was thankful I didn't have to deliver to him since I'd already been to Tabor Architects, where I delivered all his mail together. I knew it was okay when we'd been dating, but now that we weren't, I was sure it wasn't legal to deliver his personal mail there. I made a mental note that I would no longer do that and keep all of it professional.

I stood at the top of the street and looked down at the row of cottage-style homes that were only on the right side of the dead-end street. These were the first homes built in the settlement when they discovered Sugar Creek Gap, claiming it as a mill town. All the houses were two-story homes with a family room, a bedroom, a bath, and a kitchen on the first floor. The second floor was like a little loft bedroom. Each house had a small covered porch along the front with three concrete steps leading up to it.

We all had chain-link fences and a gate to enter the small grassy front yard.

"It's 'bout time you got here!" Harriette Pearl hollered from the front porch of her house, where she and the following three neighbors, who I lovingly referred to as the Front Porch Ladies, were all gathered on the two wooden swings hanging from Harriette's porch. "We was 'bout to put out an all-points bulletin on you."

I couldn't help but chuckle when I let myself in her front gate and walked up the walkway to see them.

"You even brought out the scanner?" I pointed to the police scanner she had sitting on a little wire table with the antennas stretched out like two long bunny ears.

"We were worried something happened to you." Ruby Dean, the neighbor who lived next door to Harriette, tsked. "It wouldn't be unusual for you to put yourself in a sticky situation."

"Mmhmmm, maybe another murder and all." Gertrude Stone shrugged. "I was telling Ruby that I'd been worried about you since Mac cheated."

"No, I don't want no mac and cheese." Ruby shook her head.

"Mac and cheese?" Gertrude snarled. "I said Mac cheated!" she yelled at Ruby. "Turn up your ears!"

They bantered back and forth about Ruby's hearing getting worse while I spoke up over them.

"Mac didn't cheat." That was the last rumor I wanted to be added to the rumor mill around our small town. "We decided we were better friends."

"Friends do things together." Millie Barnes gestured to the other three ladies. "And I've got my Elk's meeting with my friends." She, in her none too subtle way, was trying to get around to asking if I had her dessert from the Wallflower. "And I've not seen you and Mac even so much as look over yonder way for each other."

"We are busy just like you." I took the bag off my shoulder and took out her box before I got to their mail bundles. "And from what I hear, you're going to have some wonderful slices of smoky summer sausage and grits casserole today for your Elk's meeting."

"I can't thank your mom enough for being so kind and baking this for us. The ladies love it, and so do I. We talk all other nine months out of the year how we can't wait for summer to roll around and have some of this summer casserole." She opened the box and quickly shut it when Gertrude tried to get a look-see. "If you'd join the club like I've asked you to over and over, then you'd be getting a slice today."

"I ain't got no time to join any club." Gertrude snapped.

"Because you're too busy watching your soap opera," one of the ladies mumbled, creating all sorts of feathers being ruffled and each one of them pointing out different flaws in the others.

"I'd love to stay and referee, but I've got to go let Buster out to potty before I head on over to the neighborhood." I handed each of them their stack of mail and told them I'd see them later. "And I need to see Gerome before he leaves for the day."

"What's up with him?" Harriette was the ringleader of the Front Porch Ladies. She was the nosiest too.

"Nothing. He's the mail carrier for the garage, and I have a certified letter for Simon that was slipped into my bag by accident. It's certified, so I'm sure Simon is waiting for it."

Harriette and the gals knew all too well about waiting for mail. They loved getting mail and were always waiting for me.

"Poor guy. He is a kind young man." Harriette's lips pursed as she shook her head like he was heading to the sweet hereafter. "Never met a stranger. Always called me by name. Asked about my neighbors."

"Is there something wrong with Simon?" I lifted the bag onto my shoulder and waited at the bottom step to hear her reply.

If someone was sick or if there was some sort of scandal, Harriette would know. I swear that church telephone chain was just a license to gossip.

"You know how stories spread around here, which I didn't want to believe, but when I saw him over at the General Store, I knew the rumors were true." Harriette's lips turned down. She lifted her hand up in the air and crumpled up her fingers. "He's got some sort of early arthritis."

"Is that what it is?" Millie asked. "Kay Tedle said she'd seen him at a restaurant one day, and he could hardly pick up his fork to feed himself. It was awful."

I listened to the older women banter about the various things they heard from the rumor mill without even knowing what was actually wrong with Simon Little. Living in a small town, I knew that everyone always suspected the worse when it came to an illness.

Like this tale of Simon Little. Harriette said he's got some form of arthritis. But when she heard Millie say something about not being able to feed himself, I could see her wheels turning like he had something worse.

I was trying hard not to diagnose the young man, though I

was curious to ask Gerome since he did see Simon a few days a week, if not on a daily basis.

"I don't know about none of that, but I do know I've got to get going," I said.

"You be sure to tell us about what you find out." A smile curled up on Harriette's mouth because she knew I'd be checking into all of this gossip. "'Cause we all know how you have a way with folks and finding out the truth."

"Why, Harriette Pearl, if I didn't know better, you're saying I am a tad bit nosey." I winked and waved behind my back as I headed down the street, passing the next few houses because they belonged to the Front Porch Ladies.

The house next to me was owned by Mac and was a rental that'd been sitting empty for a few months. I wasn't sure, but I think Mac had been a little hesitant, considering what'd happened there a while back, which was another story for a different time.

When I'd moved to town from the farmhouse, I was looking forward to having a nice neighbor who I could talk over the fence to and share vegetables from my fancy garden boxes with.

"Buster," I called into the house when he wasn't at the door to greet me. The chocolate lab sounded like a horse galloping down the hallway, and he skidded around the corner with his tail looking like a whirligig that'd fallen from a tree. "You must've been taking a good nap."

I put the mail carrier bag on the floor in the family room so he didn't bowl me over with his excitement. With a few good rubs and kisses, he was ready to go do his business. While he was outside, since it was a lovely afternoon, I took my time before letting him back in and made myself a little salad to help curb my hunger.

"How are you today, Rowena?" I asked the lazy feline, who was rolled over on her back with her paws in the air like she had no care in the world. She shouldn't. She lived the life. "I hear your brother scratching at the door."

As soon as she heard me open the screen door, she darted back to the bedroom where she'd stay until the coast was clear, or at least until she heard me open the to-go box Mom had sent them once Buster had sniffed it out and reminded me it was in the mailbag.

"Your granny loves you two so much." I put the box on the counter, took a few pinches of food, and put some in each of their bowls. "Be good, kiddos. I'll be late because I'm meeting Julia at the doctor's office."

My insides churned with giddiness at the thought of playing with baby Clara while Julia was at her appointment, even if it was in the lobby of the doctor's office. Any time spent with her was well worth it.

"You look like you're far off." Monica Reed was behind the counter of the post office when I walked through the front door. "Whatcha thinking about?" She had her elbows planted on the counter with her hands cradling her chin.

"Clara." The name always put a huge smile on my face. "I am ready to get this last loop finished so I'm not late to Julia's doctor's appointment, where I'll get to watch my baby girl."

"My goodness, Bernie, I never thought I'd see the day when you turned into a girly woman." Gerome was right on time and grabbing a few of the plastic bins to throw in his truck.

I laughed.

"Monica, Bernie here is a boy's mom to the core." He winked. "Grandma looks good on you."

"Maw-maw," I told him with a hard nod, trying to wear the name with pride since Grady and Julia had told me that was what they were going to teach Clara to call me. It would've been my last choice, but I'd embraced it or, really, forced myself to embrace the name.

"Maw-maw Bernie." Monica cackled.

"Before I forget." I dropped my mailbag on the counter and opened it to get the certified letter. "There was a certified letter in my second loop for Simon Little at the mechanic shop. I did try to deliver it to him since I'm running early, but he wasn't there. I told Nick to let him know I would give it to you."

"Sure." Gerome walked over and waited for me to get it.

"I swear I put it in the side pocket." I continued to search through the mailbag. All the second loop mail was gone, and the only thing in there was a bag of duck pellets. I knew I'd put the letter in the front side pocket, but it was empty.

I took my hands out of the bag and stood there a second, retracing my steps.

"I delivered the mail to the Front Porch Ladies, then I went home to let Buster out." I snapped my fingers and stopped talking after I realized what I bet happened. "My mom had given me some scraps for the dogs, I bet when Buster was all up in my bag, he must've scratched out the letter. I bet it's on my floor at home." I let out a long sigh. "I'll come in early tomorrow and bring it in for you to give to him."

"No problem." Gerome grabbed another plastic bin filled with mail and stuck it on top of another one, picking both of them up at once. "I'll see you two cool cats tomorrow."

"Bye!" Monica and I called out in unison.

"And I've got to grab my third loop." I hurried to the back of the post office where it was employees only and filled my bag, heading out with a little jig and with the thought that I'd soon be playing with the sweetest little girl in the world.

CHAPTER 5

The doctor's building was actually next to the post office, and I'd been so quick to deliver the mail to finish my day, I'd decided to drop off my mailbag and leave it in my locker at the post office instead of fooling with it at Julia's appointment.

I only wanted to focus on Clara and not worry about keeping up with the work bag.

"I can't thank you enough, Maw-maw." Julia handed me the little pumpkin seat with Clara in it.

"Julia," I gasped when I noticed the little blond curls. "Her hair." Just looking at Clara brought tears to my eyes. "She looks just like you."

"Can you believe it? She's starting to get some little features." Julia reached down and adjusted the little blanket over Clara. "She's got Grady's lungs, though," she teased.

"He did have a nice set on him when he was a kid and hungry." I'm sure she was so sick and tired of me telling her stories about Grady as a baby.

"And that's when she acts like him." She took the baby bag,

unzipped it, and pointed to the inside straps holding the bottle. "I put in a bottle because soon she'll wake up and want to eat."

"I've got this." I was confident.

Julia and I sat there chitchatting about various things, and I could tell she was avoiding the topic on everyone in our family's mind... Mac. One of the main reasons for her checkup was to see if the doctor would clear her to go back to work. It wasn't her OBGYN that had an issue; it was the family doctor who wanted to make sure Julia's blood pressure had returned to normal since it was the cause for why Clara was born so prematurely.

When they called Julia back to the exam room, I couldn't help but give a few little shakes to the pumpkin seat in hopes Clara would wake up. I couldn't wait to see if she had Grady's big brown eyes. Julia's blond hair and his eyes would make the prettiest combination. But anything looked pretty on Clara.

The door to the exam rooms opened, and I looked up.

"Hey, Simon." The excitement exuded from me. "I'm so glad to see you. I've been thinking about you all day."

"Hey, Mrs. Butler." He walked over, and I couldn't help but notice how his pointer finger and his middle finger of both hands seemed to be curled into his palm. "Is that Grady's baby?"

"Clara Butler." My voice ran up an octave. "Isn't she precious?"

"A doll baby." He walked over and looked down at her. I took a closer look at his hands.

"Do you want to hold her?" I blurted out, thinking that she'd wake up if he said yes.

"No, ma'am." He held up his hands. "I can't do much holding on to anything right now."

"Oh no. Are you okay?" Goodness, I bet Harriette was right. He had to have some sort of terrible arthritis.

"I've got some sort of disease called Dupuytren's contracture." He held out his hands and tried to open his fingers then pointed to the tendon in his palm.

"Arthritis?" I asked.

"No, ma'am." He tapped his palm. "You can feel my tendon right here is tight like concrete. These are nodules that have created a stiffness and loss of full extension which brings my fingers in, making it look like arthritis. Right now, the only thing I can do is have surgery."

"How did you injure both hands?" I continued to look back and forth, then felt one of his palms after he gestured me to. They were so tight and hard.

Poor kid. So young.

"Not any injury. I just started to get this tightness in my hands while I was working on the cars, and so I came to the doctor. I was initially treated for carpal tunnel. Then I went to physical therapy, was treated for arthritis, then got the Dupuytren's diagnosis." He frowned, shaking his head and looking at his hands. "It's been a struggle not being able to work. It's depressing. I never thought I'd be twenty-seven and relying on my parents for help. I should be like Grady. Wife, kid, and doing what I love."

"I'm so sorry." I could feel his pain. It radiated through his eyes. "Is there anything I can do?"

"No, ma'am." He was just as polite as could be. "What was it that made you think of me today?" he asked, jarring me back to his letter.

"I stopped by the garage because there was a certified letter for you accidentally stuck in my mail carrier bag." I looked around for my bag, though I knew it wasn't in there. "Gosh. I forgot I dropped my bag off at the post office before I came over here to meet Julia for her appointment. Anyways, I told Gerome I'd give it to him tomorrow morning, and I also told Nick to tell you I was there."

"Do you know who it's from?" he asked.

"Patent office." I pretend to accidentally nudge the pumpkin seat in hopes Clara would hurry and wake up. No luck.

"Oh yeah," Simon gasped and happily sighed. It warmed me up inside to see his light turn on. "I've been waiting to see if I got a patent on this motorcycle part because it would really help if I could sell it and pay the surgery cost so my parents didn't have to."

"Nick mentioned something about that." I watched as the smile melted from his lips and his eyes clouded over with worry.

"You showed Nick the letter?" he asked.

"No. He asked if he could sign, and I showed him the envelope had your name on it for signature, so I couldn't give it to him." My eyes narrowed. "Is there something wrong?"

"No, ma'am." His chest heaved as he sucked in a deep breath. "Grady's baby sure is cute. You be sure to tell him I saw her."

He took off like a jet out of the doctor's office, and not too long after, Julia emerged from the exam room hallway with a paper in her hand.

"Already finished?" I pouted. "She never once woke up."

About that time, Clara burst out crying and so did Julia.

"Oh dear." I didn't know who to comfort first. Well, actually... I did, and I scooped her into my arms. "Julia, it's okay, what's wrong?" I rocked the pumpkin seat with the toe of my shoe, soothing Clara for a moment.

"Doctor Hunter won't clear me to go back to work, and if I don't get some peace, I'm going to lose my mind." She cried on my shoulder. "I'm so tired. Going back to work I can at least rest my eyes when Mac is gone in the afternoon."

I patted her back and let her talk out all the stress right there in the reception room, remembering exactly how hard it was to adjust to being a mom.

A few hours later and a little mentally exhausted, Iris and I were right back on that darn yoga mat in the most uncompromising position while I whispered between aches and moans how I was going to let Monica Reed take one day a week for my third loop while I cared for Clara so Julia could get out of the house, or bring Clara to my house while Julia slept at hers. Plus, I'd intended on talking to Grady about it.

"Poor gal. I bet it's hard." Iris had twisted at the waist, hugging her tented knee to her chest.

"Ladies," Peaches said, interrupting our conversation. "You get more benefits from yoga class if you also use this time mentally for yourself. Gossip later."

I gave her a flat look and slowly untwisted from the right, going into the same twist on the left and getting a good view of Lucy Drake in yet another new tight-fitting yoga outfit.

The rest of the class, I refused to let myself get all worked up about Lucy. I'd secretly wished Peaches would kick her out like she'd done Sarah, but no luck. I got lost in a daydream of wearing the shirt China was going to make for me and Lucy being jealous of me.

"Wake up." Iris nudged me. "You've got to stop falling asleep because your snoring is getting louder and louder."

"What?" I blinked awake and dragged my hand along the drool that'd dripped down my chin.

"You know you should go to the doctor about sleep apnea." Lucy Drake smiled and trotted past us with her fancy yoga mat rolled up under her arm.

"Why don't you jar me awake when I start to fall asleep?" I glared at Iris, filled with embarrassment.

"Because I'm busy worrying about myself not falling asleep." Iris grunted when she pushed herself up to stand.

"Sorry about all this, Peaches." I stood up.

"Don't you worry about it. I'm so glad your body is responding exactly the way it needs to so you can find rest. If you're falling asleep, you must be comfortable." She walked into the front of the spa. Everyone had already left the studio. "Want a drink?"

To my surprise, she tugged a big bottle of bourbon from underneath the counter along with three shot glasses.

"One for you, you, and me." She referred to me and Iris as she made the two-finger pour shots.

"No thanks." I put my hand out in front of me. "Are you okay?"

"What? Can't I have a little downtime? You use yoga; I'm using bourbon." She double fisted my shot glass and hers before she downed both.

Iris didn't miss a beat. She grabbed the one for her and gulped it right down.

"Weeee-doggie, just what I needed to get tonight's baking done." Iris smacked her lips together.

"Want to join me for another one?" Peaches wiggled the bourbon bottle in the air.

"No thanks. I want to bake, not lie on the bakery floor." Iris waved behind her and off she went.

"Sure you don't want one?" she asked me and refilled all three glasses.

"No, but I do want to know what's going on. This isn't like you." I didn't know Peaches very well, but well enough to know her to never drink like this. Maybe a cocktail here and there when I'd see her out and about, but not at her place of business.

"Let's just say that Simon and Sarah have got me a little turned up sideways," she confessed and sucked down another shot. "I didn't think it was going to bother me as much as it has. He came to see me this afternoon, and I was shocked at how fast his disease has progressed."

"I saw him at the doctor's office. He told me." I could see

anger in Peaches's face and wondered if she needed to take her own advice about her yoga class's benefits.

"He told you about us?" She got super defensive and on edge as if there were a big secret.

"No. He told me about the disease." I wanted to ask about them, but it certainly wasn't my place unless she wanted to disclose it.

"Oh." She threw down the last shot as her head tilted back, letting the bourbon slide down her throat. "Hopefully, the surgery will help. I need you to take this."

She picked up a package off the floor and put it on the counter.

"It was delivered to my house today. I know it's from Simon, and I can't accept it." She had written "return to sender" all over the box. She pushed it toward me.

"I can't take it tonight since it's work, but leave it here, and I'll get it in the morning when I deliver your mail." I patted her hand. "I'm going to go. Do you think you're going to be okay?"

"I'm fine. I've got China's bag of clothes to sort through, so I'm going to spend the night here on one of the massage tables." She must've seen the look on my face. "Don't worry. I do it all the time."

"Okay, but if you ever need someone to talk to, please find me. Not a bottle." I picked up the bourbon bottle and set it back down.

"I'll be fine." She rolled her eyes and laughed. "You keep working on your flexibility. Rest. Don't let Lucy Drake intimidate you."

"That noticeable?" I shrugged, laughing. "It looks like me and you are in the same boat," I joked and headed out the door.

CHAPTER 6

No matter how much Peaches Partin preached about how good yoga was, encouraging me to stick with it because it would help me sleep, it started to sound like a lot of bull malarkey to me. Unless she meant the end of class when she had us lie down and put a nice, warm, cozy blanket over us, which I fell asleep to every single time.

I wanted the full night's sleep I used to get when Grady was little and Richard was alive. Instead of dwelling on how much my body ached from yoga class and the tossing and turning all night, I got myself up and got ready for work. I decided to head on over to the garage early this morning, after my first loop, to see if Simon was there yet. When I'd gotten home last night, the certified letter was on the floor exactly where I thought it might've been when I couldn't find it in my bag.

"Buster," I called out from the front door with his leash in my hand, figuring it was early and he'd love to accompany me on the walk from our house to the post office to get my first loop, then head to the garage to drop off the letter, and then go back to the post office to get my second loop of mail.

From what Lucy Drake had said on the early morning radio weather update, which made me a little happy she was at work and not shacking up down the street with Mac, it was going to be a really cool morning but temperatures were going to rise as the day went on.

As soon as Buster saw his leash, he was raring to go. His hard tail whacked me a few times.

"You be a good girl," I told Rowena, who sat a good distance back so she wouldn't be in the line of danger, Buster's tail. She blinked a few slow blinks like she was telling me how happy she was to have the house to herself.

With the leash clipped on Buster's collar, we were ready to go. The duck paddled around the foot of the bridge that connected Main Street to the veterinary clinic across the street from the post office.

"What on earth?" I gasped when I saw a few of the sheriff's deputies' Jeeps parked along the side of the post office. All the lights were on inside, which never happened until Monica opened the service center.

"Come on." I tugged on Buster's leash to get him to stop sniffing around the vet clinic's bushes and ran across Main Street to the back of the parking lot where none of the LLV drivers were going around their vehicles doing their morning assessments of the trucks.

That told me something was really wrong.

"Monica, what's going on?" I'd found Monica near the taped-off area by the door. The kind like the police or, in our case, sheriff's taped-off area that meant there was a crime.

"Someone has broken in to the post office." Her voice cracked. She gnawed on her already short fingernails. "I had no idea when I let myself in this morning until I had flipped on the lights for y'all to see when you come through the back door." She bent down and started to pat Buster.

Both of us stopped when we heard another car pull up. It was Sheriff Angela Hafley.

"What on earth did they steal? Stamps?" I joked, trying to make light of the situation since I could see she was relaxing a little with Buster's help. He was so good at calming people. Even before I inherited him, when I'd show up to his house, he always could tell when I was having a bad day. Just as soon as I'd drop the mail off at his house for his owner, I instantly felt good. Maybe I should make him a helper dog. I put the thought in the back of my head to ask Vivian Tillett, the director of the nursing home, if they had any sort of program like that.

"I have no idea what they wanted." She let out a long sigh.

"They?" I asked, thinking more than one.

"I don't know. By the time I realized someone had broken the glass on the door, I ran out and called the sheriff's department." She continued to pat Buster as Sheriff Hafley walked up.

"Mornin', ladies." Angela stuck her hand out for Buster to smell before he gave her the go ahead to pet him all over. "I guess we have someone who just couldn't wait for their mail to be delivered."

"Is that a joke or is that what's happened?" I asked, not able to read Angela's body language. I had gotten really good at that, but it was still pretty dark out, and I'd yet to have ten cups of coffee, so I was blaming lack of sleep.

Dang yoga.

"Bernie, I'm joking. I have no idea yet why someone would break in, but I'm guessing to do something so drastic, it would be in anticipation of receiving a letter possibly." She had a point, I guess. She directed her next words to Monica. "Can I get a quick statement from you?"

"Yeah, sure," Monica agreed and followed Angela to the sheriff's car, passing Gerome on the way.

"Crazy stuff." Gerome shook his head. "Gonna make me late,

and my boy has a Little League soccer game this afternoon that I wanted to make it to."

Every morning the lifelong vehicle mail carriers had to go over their mail trucks pretty thoroughly. If they found something wrong, they'd turn in the repairs and hopefully get those done. That's why Nick was there yesterday morning, which reminded me of the letter I had for Simon.

"If it's any time off, I'm more than happy to give the garage their mail since I still have Simon's letter." I talked and watched as the deputies continued to walk back and forth with updates on what was going on inside to Angela and the postmaster general. "Speaking of Simon, I had no idea he had that terrible disease where the tendons in his hands contract."

"Poor guy. He gets his medication mailed from Canada because it's cheaper. Sad thing is that it takes longer, so he's been waiting on his refill for a week. I bet he's out of medication too." Gerome's eyes grew big, he slid his chin to the side, tilted his head, and looked at me with a look of disbelief. "Do you think he broke in here to see if his meds were here?"

"No. How could he?" I questioned. "He can't hold anything to break in."

"I never thought about that." He sighed. "But someone wanted something."

Both of us turned our attention to the door when we noticed a deputy had walked out with a mail carrier bag. The deputy walked over to Angela's car. She got out, and they had a little discussion. I watched as she turned her gaze to me. She lifted her chin in the air slightly like she was talking about me, making the deputy look my way. His eyes caught mine, and in an instant, I knew the bag was mine.

"Giiirl, it looks like they got your bag. And I'm not sticking around to see what is up with that." Gerome took off toward a group of LLVers and left me and Buster to fend for ourselves.

"I'm guessing that's my bag." I didn't bother making small talk with the deputy. "And somehow it's tied into this break-in?"

"Yes, ma'am." He was very polite. "It appears the person who broke in had the most interest in your open locker. All the shelves were torn out, and as you can see, the lining of your bag is ripped as well as the pockets."

"It looks like someone got angry." A chill ran up my leg, and it wasn't from the cool morning.

"I'm going to need a list of names and addresses of all the customers you see on a daily basis." He rattled off a few more things he was going to need.

"You can get all that information from the postmaster or Monica Reed, who is with Angela right now." I reached for my bag; he pulled it back.

"Sorry, evidence. There could be fingerprints on it. It's a federal offense to break in to a post office." He didn't tell me anything I didn't already know since we had to learn all of that in training. "Have any of your customers acted strange lately or asked about packages they are waiting on?"

"Not that I can think of, but it's pretty early, so my brain isn't functioning at full capacity." I tapped my head. "Plus, Doc Hunter did mention something about me having some white specs due to an old brain."

His brows dipped, his face contorted, he opened his mouth, and then shut it as if he were trying to process what I'd said.

"But I'll think on it and get back to you." I helped make it easy for him.

"Yeah. Just call the sheriff's department if you think of something." He took a few steps back.

"Are we going to get to work soon?" I asked in hopes I could start and possibly help Gerome out if I did get finished quickly.

"It's gonna be a few to clear out the scene. Maybe an hour or so. We called down at WSCG to let Lucy Drake know so she can broadcast it on her show this morning." He smiled. "Thank goodness for her and her show. Folks around here just love her show."

"Mmhhmmm." I tugged on Buster's leash. "Let's go."

I didn't bother telling anyone I was heading down to the gas station. I figured I could get down there and deliver Simon's letter to him before I walked back to the post office in about an hour.

The sunlight was starting to illuminate Sugar Creek Gap, and though the garage was on the outskirts of downtown, there was a nice sidewalk along the road the entire way. It was built a few years ago when they had built the new streetscape with the extra grant money our town received from the state. It was a complete overhaul with a new paved road, sidewalks, lights, and some buildings that had been refaced.

The grant was to keep the town up so it could stay on the historical registry. When you could claim your town as a part of the state's history, all sorts of money was thrown to preserve it. Being an old mill town with a working mill definitely qualified Sugar Creek Gap, making me super thankful for the redone sidewalks. Especially this early in the morning.

The lights under the gas station roof where the pumps were located were on and shined brightly. The garage door was wide open, and I could hear music coming from the radio or should I say the sweet sound of Lucy Drake's seductive voice dripping through the speaker of the old transistor. I stopped when I heard her talking and could see through the office window that Simon was in there working at the desk. I let Buster's leash go, and he trotted into the garage like he'd done before when we'd stopped to get gas or even just take a nice long weekend walk.

Good morning, y'all. This is your gal Lucy Drake with an important announcement from Sheriff Angela Hafley. Please be patient with your mail carriers today. The post office was broken in to, and though they do not believe any mail was stolen since the door to that area of the post office wasn't compromised, the sheriff and her deputies are working diligently to make sure everything is safe and secure down there before they let our mail carriers have their route mail. Also, the lobby will remain closed as well, so don't be going down there and sweet-talking Monica Reed to grab your stack of mail because we all know that they are gonna be swamped. So be sure to love up on your mail carrier today. Even throw them a little treat or two.

Hello caller, you're on Coffee Chat with Lucy. Do you have a question?

Aw, Lucy. Me and my family just love you. You sure are as pretty as you sound.

Her giggle made me just about nauseous.

Why, aren't you the sweetest. What's your question?

Do you figure it was someone who broke in to the post office because there might be something important being held up in there? I mean, we are only an hour or so from Fort Knox, and it's all full up on gold.

"Where do they get these callers?" I asked Simon as I headed into the office knowing he'd just heard exactly what I'd heard. Buster had jumped up and put two paws on Simon's chair, swiveling it a little. "Buster. You can push him away." I smacked my hand to my thigh. "Buster! Down!" I moved my attention to the certified letter in my back pocket, and when I looked up to give it to Simon, his chair had turned to face me. "Simon?" I questioned when I saw his eyes were open, his face was grey, and his lips were blue. "Simon!" I screamed when I realized he wasn't moving or breathing.

I took a few steps forward, hitting an empty bottle of pills with my shoe. It twirled away under the desk.

I threw the letter on the desk and immediately felt for a pulse. Nothing.

I reached into my other pocket and quickly dialed 911.

"Hurry. The gas station. Simon Little isn't breathing." My heart beat rapidly. "I think..." I gulped. "I think he's dead."

CHAPTER 7

Unfortunately, this wasn't the first time I'd found a dead body, and I knew to leave well enough alone by grabbing Buster's leash and slowly backing out of the office, where we tried not to disturb anything.

I'm not going to lie, before I crept out the way I had come in, I did take a little look-see around to try and see if there was a tad bit of foul play, even though I wouldn't think so. It all looked as if Simon had drunk the entire bottle of bourbon that was sitting on the desk next to a glass with a little drip of golden-brown liquid settled in the bottom.

There also looked like there was some sort of document that'd been typed out on the computer. I tried to squint but couldn't make out what it said unless I took a step closer. I already had the heebie-jeebies from how close I was standing to a dead body, and I wasn't about to take another step forward.

I gripped Buster's leash tight, making him come as close to my legs as he possibly could, in fear he'd go rogue and start sniffing around.

We waited outside of the office near the gas pumps for just a few minutes before I saw the red-and-white sheriff lights flashing in the pink sky of the early morning sunrise. Angela Hafley's sheriff's car was the only department car with red-and-white lights. The deputy cars and Jeeps only had red lights.

If Angela was coming, there had to be a question on Simon's death, or she would've stayed down at the post office with the federal offense crime scene since that had never happened in Sugar Creek Gap. Someone dying was not an everyday occurrence, but it was something that did happen.

"And look who it is." There was a long pause in Angela's disposition when she noticed it was me.

"Yes," I said, deciding to play along, "Buster decided to join me."

"You know I'm not talking about Buster." She reached into her car and pulled out the official sheriff's round brown hat with the Sugar Creek Gap logo embroidered on it.

That's when I knew Angela meant serious business, not that finding a dead body wasn't serious. It was. But when she wore the hat, it was very serious. There was a deputy with her, and he'd already gone inside the office. He came out to confirm Simon was dead, so they didn't need to call the life squad.

While he did all the talking on the walkie-talkie attached to his sheriff's brown uniform shirt, Angela decided to question me.

"Why is it that you're like a coon dog and can sniff out a dead body better than they can sniff out a raccoon?" Even though she asked the question, I knew better than answering because she didn't want an answer. It was her way of telling me to back off.

"A gift, I guess." I shrugged and let the grip on Buster's leash lessen because he was doing his wiggle and jiggle to let Angela pat him. She did.

"What am I going to find in there?" she asked, her eyes hooded under the large round rim of her hat.

"Simon Little. Eyes open. Empty handle of bourbon. Some

sort of note on the computer monitor." I replayed the scene in my head. "Oh! An empty prescription bottle that I accidentally kicked under his desk when I went into the office to give him the letter." I patted around my body. "The letter!"

"What letter?" Angela eyed me.

"The reason I'm here is because Simon had a certified letter that was accidentally put in my mailbag yesterday." I rolled my hand in front of me, deciding not to tell her how Buster had gone through my bag to get to the food my mom had given me on my route, and cut to the chase. "Long story short, I still had the letter to give to Gerome this morning, but since we couldn't get our mail loops until later, Buster and I walked down to give him the letter. Certified letter. But I bet the pills are for his disease." My mind wandered off. "I told him I had it when I saw him at the doctor's office yesterday."

"You mean you had a certified letter for Simon Little in your mailbag. The mailbag that someone who broke in to the post office was very interested in seeing? But they didn't get the letter because you had it at home and brought it down here today?"

"When you put it that way, do you think all of this is tied?" My jaw dropped, my eyes grew big, and my mouth dried.

"Do you think it's all by accident?" she asked and turned her head toward the office. "Where's the letter?"

"I dropped it on his desk when I went to feel for a pulse. Then I called you." I pushed back the thought that this was a murder and it had to do something with that patent.

"Then you looked around?" Her eyes narrowed like they always did when she let me know I'd overstepped my bounds.

"I didn't walk around. I searched around with my eyes, but never tied the two together. Two, meaning the post office and Simon's murder." The disbelief that this could happen curled in my head.

"Whoa." Angela put her hands up. "I never said this was a

murder. Maybe Simon went looking for the letter since he knew you had it. When he couldn't find it, maybe he took his medication while drinking a bourbon. Accidentally killing himself." She let out a long deep sigh. "But we won't know anything until I get in there and assess the scene. So why don't you wait right here?"

"I didn't do anything. I didn't touch anything." I wondered why she wanted me to stay. "Can't I just come down to the station later today?"

"No." She pointed at me like I would Buster. She commanded, "Stay."

"I guess we are staying." I sat down on the curb of one of the gas pumps and had Buster sit between my legs. I cradled him to me while more and more sheriff's deputies and the WSCG radio van, where they did mobile live news, drove to the scene.

None other than Lucy Drake hopped out in the cutest pair of cropped skinny jeans and red short-sleeved pullover sweater. Her makeup was on point, her lipstick matched her sweater, and her hair lay in loose waves down her back.

She pointed and gestured to the audio man to follow her. I twisted around so she didn't see me, but apparently, she saw me before she got out of the van.

"Bernie"—her peppy voice made me cringe—"What's going on? I was doing my broadcast, and when I saw the sheriff zooming out of downtown, followed by all the deputies, I told Rod we had to jump on this." She turned to the guy in the skintight black tee shirt and equally tight jeans, who had sleeve tattoos on both arms.

"Yeah, we love a good sheriff's case." He winked at Lucy, which struck me as odd. Her schoolgirl giggle was even more strange.

"So, what's the gig? I want to go live." Her eyes popped open, and a smile curled on her perfectly lined lips before her lids slowly and seductively lowered.

"I don't know." I shrugged then pushed away the microphone she'd shoved in my face. I didn't like the last few times she did this to me, and now I really didn't like it, considering the deep feelings I was harboring about her.

"Of course, you do. It was on the police dispatch that you called in that Simon Little was dead." She was good at listening to the police scanner. "If the entire sheriff's department is here, that means it's more than just dead." She reached over and tapped Rod on the arm. "Start the remote."

He pushed all sorts of buttons on a gadget he took out of the bag that had been strapped across his body.

"This is Lucy Drake with breaking news." She talked into the microphone, causing the radio in the garage to echo her voice. "Simon Little, owner of the mechanic shop, has been found dead in the gas station office. We are here with Bernadette Butler, who actually called in the emergency to the sheriff's dispatch." She took that darn microphone and slid it back over in front of my mouth.

I clenched my jaw and gave her a good hard stare. She brought the microphone back to her mouth.

"Bernie, do you mind telling us why you were here this morning? I don't recall you being the mail carrier for the garage, and I believe all mail has been put on hold for delivery today until further notice." She stuck the microphone back in my face and then decided to really try to get me to talk. "Is this a related case? Did you know something about it and come to warn Simon? I can only conclude Simon had something to do with the post office break-in. Or maybe the two of you did it..."

If I didn't stop her crazy rant, I knew she'd keep going with all sorts of conspiracy theories.

My phone in my back pocket started to chirp messages from

people who I knew were listening to Lucy's made-up, but not off base, tales about what was going on.

"I am..." I started to say before Angela Hafley cleared her throat a distance behind me.

"I will be more than happy to give the listeners a statement once we know something." Angela looked down her nose at the microphone Lucy had now stuck in her face. "As for Bernadette Butler, we had told her at the post office that we'd let them know in an hour if they could start to deliver their mail routes, so she had informed me that she and her dog were going to go for a walk. When Mrs. Butler walked past the gas station, she noticed Mr. Little was here and came in to tell him hello like we all do when we see our friends in our tight-knit community." Angela clasped her hands in front of her and looked at me. "If you'll excuse Mrs. Butler, a deputy is going to take her back to the post office where I'm very proud to announce the mail carriers will be able to start their workday."

Angela gestured for me to follow the deputy, and I gladly accepted the invitation and was very appreciative for the ride.

"Sheriff Hafley wanted me to tell you that you are to keep your mouth shut about the letter Simon had left behind for his family and, for that matter, to keep your mouth and observations to yourself as this is an ongoing investigation that has to do with the federal offense of him breaking in to the post office." The officer gave me specific instructions as he drove me downtown to the post office. He threw the Jeep in gear. "You are to come to the department after work and give your full official statement. Do you understand, Mrs. Butler?"

"Yes." I opened the door and pulled Buster out behind me.

CHAPTER 8

There's a saying about small town and gossip. I believed it went something like this: small towns, small minds, big mouths, big rumors. And, boy, were the rumors flying all around like bats at dusk. And, of course, the gossip was ahead of the police, making me a very popular mail carrier.

"And you don't know if it was related?" Vince Caldwell, the retired FBI agent and full-time resident of the senior living condominiums at Sugar Creek Gap Nursing Home and Senior Living, had asked as soon as I walked up with his mail in my hand.

"Good morning to you too." I looked over at him patting the open space on the front porch swing where I found him every single morning with the newspaper in his hands. Today, he had an extra cup of coffee.

Could've been because I was more than an hour late to our morning rendezvous, or he wanted a little information, and coffee was a way to loosen my lips. He handed me the cup of hot steaming java.

"I figured you'd want to discuss all the muck and mess up

inside of your brain." He looked around. "But I heard Buster was with you."

"He was, and after the deputy took me back to the gas station, I knew I had a few minutes before Monica and some of the other clerks were ready for us to get our loops, and I wanted to avoid any questions, so I took him home." I held the cup in both hands.

Vince was right about one thing. I was planning on telling him all about it. He was the only one I would probably discuss it with in detail.

While we sat there, rocking on the swing and sipping our coffee, I told him everything: from hearing about Simon's disease to seeing him at the doctor's office to finding him dead at his desk.

"Do you think he killed himself?" Vince asked. It was a question I'd even asked myself.

"I don't think so, but I did know he was in pain from the tightness of his hands. He seemed pretty happy when he told me he was glad the patent letter had come through because, if he did get it, then he could sell the part and pay for the surgery to fix his hand so his parents didn't have to pay for it." I took another sip, trying to force the goose bumps off my legs though I knew it wasn't from being cold.

My mind started to play the events of yesterday that circled around the letter. My eyes darted back and forth along the concrete patio with thoughts of me talking to Nick Kirby. He really seemed taken aback by the fact there was a certified letter to Simon only.

"There goes the light bulb of our very own mail carrier sleuth." Vince's voice ticked up, and he smacked his leg.

"I don't think Simon killed himself." My voice was laced with concern. "I think Nick Kirby had a reason to kill him, and Nick Kirby knew I had the letter."

"Are you saying Nick Kirby killed Simon Little? His partner?" Vince asked.

"Yeah. And I think I need to pay him a visit." There were a lot of emotions buried in my words.

"Maybe you need to tell Angela your suspicion before you go meddling." Vince had never really acted this way toward one of my many amateur sleuthing romps around Sugar Creek Gap.

"I like to think of myself as helping not meddling." I stood up and grabbed my bag, hoisting it up onto my shoulders. "And if I'm going to do it, I've got to get all this mail delivered."

And, in record time, I did it. I'd decided that after I stuffed all the boxes at the nursing home, I'd deliver the mail to my third loop, the neighborhood, next. No one would be awake, and I could zoom past each mailbox, most of them attached to the house, which was why they needed a foot carrier. It took much longer when I delivered in the afternoon with people out gardening and fiddling around their yards, kids playing on the sidewalk, and me joining in on a good game of hopscotch or four-square was a daily summer activity.

It was my second loop where I'd spend most of my day, and I was sure to keep my ears peeled to pick up any juicy tidbits along the way.

I'd also text Angela to see if she wanted me to listen around town since she'd actually asked me to be a consultant on a previous case. She had claimed how townsfolk told me things, which they did. Everyone trusted their mail carrier. And they should. We knew about our clients more than their own families.

Especially when people worked from home. I could single out stay-at-home moms, but the work-from-home dads ordered just as much stuff through the mail they didn't want their wives to find out about. Like a good mail carrier, I kept my mouth shut... on most stuff. Or I never told the names. It was something

Iris and I loved to gossip about when I helped her in the kitchen at Pie in the Face.

Tonight wasn't any different.

"You didn't get any information from Vita?" Iris asked, referring to Vita Dickens, the dispatch operator turned deputy, who was my go-to gal for all thing secretive.

I sat on the stool next to the workstation in the middle of Iris's bakery kitchen and watched her make a homemade pie crust.

"Nope. I tried to get her attention, but my hands were empty." I lifted them in the air, both of us knowing I meant that I was without a sugary bribe for Vita.

I wasn't above bribing anyone for information. Especially when I had someone on the inside of the sheriff's department. Vita loved anything strawberry.

"I even have some slices of pan strawberry shortcake you could've taken to her." Iris took the chilled butter out of the refrigerator and added it to the dry ingredients she'd already gathered together in a bowl. She tossed it all together before she poured it all on a marble pastry board where she married the hard butter and dry ingredients over and over with a rolling pin.

"I'll be dropping the mail off tomorrow, so box it up for me before I leave tonight." I drummed my fingers on the counter and started to formulate my game plan on how I would present it to her. "Vince told me he'd also ask Colvin Batty during their pretzel betting card game tonight if he'd heard anything since it is his gas station."

A sudden burst of heat radiated from my feet. I tried to take big deep breaths like Doctor Hunter had told me to do when it felt like my legs were next to a furnace. I tried to think of a cold bath, like an ice-cold bath, with each inhale. I visualized a stream of frosty fog on the exhale.

"What's wrong?" Iris threw the empty bowl where she'd

mixed the ingredients for the crust in the sink and rushed over to me. "Are you about to pass out? The thought of the dead body getting to you?"

"No." I fanned my hands in front of me. The beads of sweat were starting to line up on my upper lip like little soldiers. "Hot flash."

"What can I do?" Iris had yet to start her change of life, and we were the same age. Something I envied about her.

"Nothing. Just taking off my shoes to let the steam release from my feet is about it, and I won't do it in your kitchen." It didn't help I still had on my work uniform and thick-soled shoes that helped with my aching feet.

"Are you kidding?" Iris bent down and tried to untie the laces. "You're my best friend, and I don't have anything out right now."

I didn't do the right Southern thing and pretend to go on and on about not doing it so she'd insist a few more times. With her permission, I used the toe of the other shoe, not bothering to untie them, and simply slipped them off, peeling back my socks.

"I think it's your toes begging to get help with that chipped-up polish." Iris's nose curled when she noticed my toenail polish wasn't the prettiest. "Dang. Now that you and Mac aren't dating, you've let your toes go to the dogs."

"Listen, I've been focused on little Clara, and she doesn't care what Maw-maw looks like." The instant relief of having the socks off was an immediate effect. "I'm letting them get good and ready to pedicure, so when Clara is old enough, we can have a girls' day."

"Really?" Iris laughed. "That's gonna be a few years from now."

"So? I've got plenty of time," I joked.

"Since we aren't too worried about men..." Iris flipped the

frosted lid off of one of her fancy cake stands, and lo and behold, she uncovered my favorite dessert.

Hummingbird cake.

"We can have a big slice." She gently picked up the three-layered cake and placed it next to me on the workstation. She grabbed two forks from the drawer, and she dug in first.

"No plates?" I questioned.

"Nope. This is for me and you," she said with a joyful tone through a mouthful of the moist creation. "Go on. I know it's your favorite. Maybe I can talk you into getting those toenails done."

I started to put my fork in the cream cheese icing and remembered Lucy Drake.

"I'm not going to do it." I put the fork down and crossed my arms.

"What?" A wail ripped through her. "Now I know something else is wrong. Dish."

"I don't know. I'm going through all these changes. I have no idea why I couldn't commit to Mac. He starts dating Lucy, who has the body of a thirty-year-old. Then I become a maw-maw when I didn't want to be named Maw-maw, but Grady loves it. Then I go to yoga, where I can't do any of the moves, and I not only have to look at Lucy, but I fall asleep and snore." I patted my stomach. "I've never snored until I put on all this extra weight over the past year."

"It's menopause. You walk every day and keep in shape. It's something we all go through, and I bet Lucy Drake is gonna be one ugly woman going through the change. Don't you remember how her own mama blew up like a balloon."

Iris always had a way of making me smile.

"That's when she started all that crazy exercise. Then she got that face-lift and those nails." Iris's eyes grew.

"Oh my gosh. I forgot about the nails!" I squealed. "I

remember sitting in church and seeing Lucy with her mom. Her mom would rake those long daggers down Lucy's dad's hairline. My mom would tell my dad that Mrs. Drake needed to get a room instead of going to church."

Iris and I nearly fell off the stool laughing so hard.

"I didn't even know what that meant until Mrs. Drake did up and leave Mr. Drake." I picked up the fork and, without even thinking about what I was doing, dug right on into that moist Hummingbird cake and took the biggest bite. "That night she left, I remember my dad telling Mom how he guessed Mrs. Drake did get that room but with another man."

"Those were the good ole days when all the gossip wasn't about us." Iris lifted a forkful of cake up in the air before she airplaned it into her mouth.

"Ain't that the truth?" I decided to follow suit and grab the biggest bite I could. "Honestly, I have to wonder if Lucy has a little of her mama's wandering eye."

Iris jerked her head up, quickly darting a heavy gaze at me.

"Yeah. Today, she showed up at the gas station with some big burly guy. They seemed to be a little too friendly with each other, and he winked at her." I gave Iris an example. "A flirty wink."

"I told Mac she wasn't..." Iris bit her lip.

"What did you tell Mac and when?" I squirmed uncomfortably on the stool.

"Listen, I just mentioned when he came in here to pick up dessert. He insisted that it was you who didn't want to carry your relationship to the next level, and I told him he needed to give you time." She frowned and looked at my face to see if I was going to be mad. "I'm only wanting you to feel better even though I'm thoroughly enjoying having you all to myself again."

"Thank you." A grateful warmth filled me inside for my good friend. "How could I be mad at you?"

"You know I love you." She reached over and nearly fell off her stool when she put her arms around me to give me the comforting reassurance I needed.

"I bet you're the reason why he stopped me today at his office. I could tell he was itching to talk to me about us, but I simply can't go there right now." It dawned on me, and I felt a little inner peace as the words left my mouth. "I guess I'm upset, not because we didn't work out, but because he was going on a date with Lucy Drake the next day." I remembered how I'd seen him at one of the Sunday night clogging events and how they danced together. "But I want him to be happy."

"I want you to be happy." She pushed back a stray strand of my hair and gave me one last hug. "Seriously, enough of that chatter. I need to know if we're going to spy on people?"

"Because I think Simon Little didn't die by his own hand?" I just had an inkling there was foul play involved.

"Yep." A big grin started at the corners of her lips, softening her face and brightening her eyes. "I mean, you did mention that you took the letter to the garage before Simon saw it. How did Nick react?"

"He really wanted me to let him sign it. He did mention they'd been working on a patent together, and I know for a fact when a patent letter is sent with two owners, both owners have to sign." I'd seen it many times with certified mail. Especially when it came from a governmental office. "Do you think Nick could've possibly asked Simon about it?"

"I don't know, but if it does come back as foul play, I'd make sure you tell Angela exactly how Nick reacted when you tried to hand deliver it to Simon." Iris was right and fed the little niggling idea that Simon's death wasn't by his own hand, but by the hand of someone else.

Someone who had a very good reason to kill him... money.

CHAPTER 9

After I'd gotten home from eating too much hummingbird cake with Iris, I took Rowena and Buster for a quick walk down Little Creek Road where the Front Porch Ladies were already tucked in to bed, so I didn't have to worry about them stopping me to gossip. I also noticed Lucy Drake's car was parked on the street in front of Mac's house and the smell from a charcoal grill wafted through the air.

When me and the fur kids hurried past Mac's house, I couldn't help but grab a sneak peek from the side of his house where he'd designed and built a very cool outdoor living area complete with a fancy grill and pizza oven. The twinkling lights along the pergola were blinking as if hundreds of fireflies were batting around. Mac loved those lights. It left me with a long deep sigh, knowing he and Lucy were probably all snuggled up on the outdoor ottoman he'd bought after I had mentioned how much I loved it when we saw it on some glitzy shop online.

"Don't you know what this means?" Lucy's voice echoed into the dark night.

"It means you're sticking your nose somewhere it doesn't belong." Mac's voice cut through the night.

"It means that if I can get a break on the headline, then I might get picked up by the Associated Press." Lucy didn't sound too happy. "It means I can finally get the break I need to be seen as a real reporter."

"You're a morning DJ." Mac wasn't very good at stroking Lucy's ego like I'm sure she wanted him to. "But you do what you want."

They appeared from the side of his house. Mac's hair was begging me to pat it down; I could see it fluffed up a little where he'd run his hands through it. He had on a gray tee shirt and his baggy jeans that fit perfectly on him. The hem scraped the grass as he walked in his bare feet. I didn't bother looking at her as I slipped Rowena into my arms and curled in Buster's leash while we tucked in front of Harriette's house by her gate. Any movement and Mac would see us.

"Mac Tabor, you know what?" Lucy Drake took a deep breath and turned around. She pointed a finger at him like she was a school principal giving him a good talkin' to. "I know you don't have any desire to take me and you beyond this little dinner here, chitchat there, coffee here. So, I'm going to go and get this lead taken care of."

"I'm sorry. You're right." Mac didn't let her fluster him. "I don't intend to have a relationship with you, other than company. So, I guess it's not fair to think we could be just friends and enjoy each other's company."

"Not at my age." Her chest lifted in her tight sweater before she shimmied her hips. "If you want that kind of relationship, I suggest you walk right on down Little Creek Road back into Bernadette Butler's house, where you did have that kind of relationship before you got bored."

Bored? My jaw dropped. Did he tell her that I bored him? The nerve! Good for her for leaving, I thought, when she got into her car and zoomed off into the night.

I stayed crouched down as the anger seethed into my veins.

"I'll show him boring," I whispered into Rowena's ear before I felt like the coast was clear and Mac had gone to his backyard.

I put Rowena back on the ground and gave Buster a little more slack in his leash so we could walk back home.

"I never said you were boring." A weird feeling of dread crawled through me when I heard Mac's voice.

I twirled around, trying not to let Buster drag me where Mac was leaning up against his side fence with a huge smile on his face.

"She said you said I was boring." I took a couple of steps closer so Buster wasn't gagging from the taut leash.

"Hey, buddy." Mac reached over the fence to pet Buster, who had jumped up so Mac didn't have to try so hard to pat him. "I'm sorry you heard that."

"I wasn't snooping." I wanted him to know I wasn't. "I'd just gotten home from the bakery and decided to take the kids for a walk." I took a few steps closer to him.

I gulped when I could smell him. He had a certain smell that always seemed to get my attention, even when I was married to Richard. It was his smell. Something that couldn't be bottled. When we'd first started to date, I remembered feeling like a ridiculous, giddy woman when he'd left his sweatshirt at the house after we'd done some remodeling, and I slept with it so I could wake up smelling him.

"What did you eat at the bakery?" He reached over and ran the pad of his thumb on my chin. "If I didn't know better..." He paused and held his thumb up in the light of the moon. "I'd think you were eating hummingbird cake without me."

"You and I both have such a soft spot for that darn cake." I couldn't help but hurt so much on the inside. There was so much history between us; it was hard to even think of any memories that didn't include him. "If you want a piece, I did bring the entire thing home with me."

"Bernie, are you asking me to come down for cake as a friend, or are you feeling what I'm feeling?" Mac had been so great at being able to get to the heart of the matter. "Because I can't take any more rejection from you. My heart aches when I go see Clara. I never wanted to take Lucy, but she hopped in the truck to go. You know I couldn't kick her out."

"I'm not sure what is between us." I didn't want to mislead him, but I did know that I didn't want to lose him again either. "I just know that seeing you with Lucy has gotten my goat."

"Now, we can't let that happen." He reached over the fence for me to take his hand. "I need you in my life. I understand you aren't ready to get remarried. But are you ready to completely open your heart up to me?"

My nose started to tingle as the beginning of tears began to line my eyelids.

"This is ridiculous." I let go of his hand and wiped the tears from my face. "We are too old to be acting like..."

"Our hearts don't know age. It only knows what we feel." He put his hand firmly on my shoulder. ""It can't tell me I'm too old to feel what I've felt for you for years or the way I feel about you now." He ran his hand up the back of my neck, drawing me close to him before he gently kissed me.

There was a little squeal coming from Harriette's house as soon as Mac bent down to kiss me. I turned to see Harriette's side window was open, her curtain flapping in the breeze.

"I guess someone interrupted that moment," Mac teased.

"Maybe we need to take it slow." I gripped the leashes and took a step away from the fence. "I'm still not changing my stance of jumping in and getting hitched."

Though it was nice to feel a little more whole seeing Mac and understanding he and Lucy weren't really an item, I still didn't know where I stood on the whole getting-married thing. I certainly didn't want to mislead him, and then we'd really be in a pickle if this entire situation repeated itself. Maybe our friendship wouldn't recover. Even though it'd been on rocky ground, we were at least kind to each other.

It was the whole "fool me once, shame on you; fool me twice, shame on me" attitude I didn't want him to have. I cared too much to lead him on with any misconceptions.

"Just to clarify..." I started to say before he put his finger up to my lips to shut me up.

"We are going to hang out like we did. I'll not even bring up marriage, but I do have to say my feelings have never changed for you since you turned me down." He took his finger from my mouth. "To clarify for you, Lucy was just company. There was no sort of hanky-panky at all."

"Was that on your end or hers?" I had to know.

"I just told you that I've never changed my feelings for you these past couple of months. I'm not going to say she'd didn't want more or elude to anything more, but I kept her at arm's length." Mac had never, ever lied to me as far as I knew. Even with him knowing Richard's secret all these years, which I never had asked about until I'd found out. Then he never lied to any of my questions. He might not have offered up any information, but that was not lying.

Still, the thought that Lucy Drake could somehow turn this whole situation around really bugged me.

"What about that piece of hummingbird cake?" He rubbed his belly.

"Alright." I gestured my head toward my end of the street and waited for him to walk out of his gate to meet me, Buster, and Rowena.

"Hey girl." He bent down and picked up the orange tabby. She purred in delight. She was such a flirt and loved him; well, she had a hankering for any man in general. But she always had the loudest purr for Mac.

"I have to know." I gnawed on my bottom lip and hoped the night darkness didn't give away my nervous facial features. "Why did Lucy take off?"

"She got a text that Simon Little's autopsy came back that he'd overdosed, and he'd left a letter, stating something about this disease and being unable to live with it." He carried Rowena all the way down the street and stopped briefly to fix the For Rent sign on the fence of the house next to mine.

It was his rental property, but it was kinda nice not having someone live next door. I guess living on the farm all those years had really settled into my soul, and it wasn't something I'd thought about when I moved. I loved the convenience of living so close to everything, especially work, but I never in a million years thought I'd have to keep my blinds closed practically half the day.

Mac's voice was a low hum in my head while he told me about what Lucy's text had said and how she was going to get a jump on the story because she wanted big-time fame. But why would she think this would give her fame?

The questions began to formulate in my head. Mac's voice was completely muted as my thoughts took over.

Had Simon Little really killed himself? He sure didn't act like he was going to do that when I saw him in the doctor's office. Then there was the certified letter. Is he the one who broke in to the post office? Did Angela Hafley get the security camera footage because the cameras around the building were never turned off?

Maybe Simon did break in to the post office, but why would he overdose when he had no idea what the patent said? Honestly, this didn't make sense to me.

"Don't you think?" Mac asked.

"Mmhhmmm." I looked over at him, smiled, and agreed to whatever it was he'd said.

"Me too. Great idea. What about that cake?" He took a little giddyup over to my gate and opened it up for me and Buster. I let Buster off the leash and let him run around the yard.

Rowena was happiest inside where she liked to sit on the back of the chair in the front room and look out the window.

"You looked deep in thought out there." Mac had always been good at reading my body language. "I've seen that look before, and I know you weren't listening to me when you agreed to what I'd said because I said how about we knock your house and my rental down to build a big house so you and I could get married and have ten kids."

"Oh." My eyes grew wide. "You said that?"

"Yep." His brows rose, and his forehead creased. "So, why don't you sit down while I cut us a couple of big pieces of cake with some milk, and you tell me what's going on in that head of yours."

This was exactly where me and Mac collided when it came to our differences in lifestyle. And this was the exact place I needed to tell him how I wasn't going to change.

"You aren't going to like this." I eased down at my kitchen table and folded my hands, resting them on top.

He worked around the kitchen to get the plates, forks, and drinking glasses ready for our special we-are-kinda-back-together treat. I'm not sure how much longer we'd be celebrating us after I told him about the investigation in my head. We'd been down this road a couple of times. That road was bumpy with a few potholes. Did he really want to do this again?

"Simon Little." His monotone laced response told me he already knew but wanted me to confirm. "Lucy told me how you were at the scene and was the one to call 911 when she heard it on the scanner, so I knew you'd already gotten involved. I think I'm safe to assume you don't think Simon did this to himself."

He poured the glasses of milk and put them on the table.

"Right." I kept a close eye on Mac's body language because in the past he had been dead set against me even thinking about snooping. That was another big issue we had.

"What are you thinking?" He calmly set the two plates on the table, handing me a fork, before sitting down. Instead of giving me the disapproving look he'd done before, he stuck his fork in the cake and scooped up a big bite.

"This is scaring me." I knew from this point forward I had to be up-front and honest since I was the one who had actually kept a few secrets from him.

"What?" He shrugged. "How I'm totally enjoying this cake?"

"You know what I'm talking about." I narrowed my eyes. "The last time you tried to really accept my gift for sleuthing..."

His head flew back as a burst of laughter escaped him.

"See. You don't take me seriously." I didn't even want to take a bite of cake. I folded my arms across my chest.

"I am taking you seriously. You said you had a gift for sleuthing, and it tickled me. You're cute." His little grin made my heart swoop up into my throat. "I like how you say it's a gift when you actually snoop around, collect clues, and try to put it together like a puzzle. That's all." He raked the edge of his fork along some of the icing that'd fallen from the cake. "Go on. I'm listening."

"I had a certified letter to Simon. When I tried to deliver it after it'd been stuck in my mailbag on accident, Nick wasn't too pleased when he'd noticed it was from the United States Patent Office."

Mac looked at me intently. There was some interest in his eyes.

I continued, "Later that day, I saw Simon at the doctor's

office, and that's when he told me about Dupuytren's contracture." I held my hands in the air to show him what Simon's fingers looked like and briefly described what the disease was about and how it had affected Simon's ability to work on any car. "That's when he told me the letter was about the patent he'd filed online for this special motorcycle bike part that would generate him a lot of money so he could afford the surgery and not take money from his parents."

"You gave him the letter." Mac took a drink of his milk.

"No. The letter was at my house under that front entrance table, long story." I decided it wasn't worth going into detail how Buster had gotten it out when sniffing out the to-go box from Wallflower Diner. "I told him I'd give it to Gerome to be delivered the next day. Which was today. But I still had the letter at home, and the person who broke in to the post office only went through my locker and my bag."

"Which meant someone wanted the letter. Possibly Simon if he was so desperate to see what the letter said. If he was in pain as you said he was, he had a prescription for the pain. Those were probably the pills Lucy said the autopsy indicated he overdosed with." Mac had started to catch on to my little theory a little too eagerly, which made me suspicious.

Why was he all of a sudden really into the whole sleuthing thing?

"Or Nick Kirby wanted to see what was in the letter, and he broke in to the post office to get it before or maybe after he killed Simon. Nick had approached him about the patent after Nick thought Simon was going to file it under both their names and even their company name." It was a good theory to test on Mac and see if he was really on board with me continuing to be who I was going to be.

The possibilities ran through my head, and I was feeling pretty good about how far my sleuthing skills had come.

Then I realized Mac was silent.

"What?" I asked him. "You are looking at me funny. And it's not the same look you gave me in the past when you told me how you didn't want me to look into things."

"I also have been without you a few months, and I have to say that I miss that quirky side of you." There was sincerity in his voice and in his body language. He reached across the table and took the fork out of my hands, clasping his hands over mine. "I told myself this morning when I tried to talk to you at my office that if I ever got a chance to be with you again, like really be with you, that I had to embrace the strong woman you are."

A lump started to form in my throat.

"You've been through so much and practically raised Grady on your own." I knew he'd recognized how much Richard was "away on business" and how alone I really was. "You have fought through so many battles, that when we decided to be an us last year"—he squeezed my hands—"I wanted to take care of you. I wanted you to have everything you've always wanted, and I wanted to give that to you. But as we went on, I noticed how you thought I was changing you, and you were right." He shrugged. "I don't want to see anything happen to you if you do get in a killer's way, but I also know that you are strong, smart, and you can handle yourself without any help from this guy."

"Are you telling me that you really are okay with all this?" I slipped my hands out from underneath his, and my finger circled my body. "And all of this." I patted my stomach. "Because my body is going through a whole lot right now, which means I'm not going to try to force myself to contort into those crazy yoga poses to look like you-know-who."

I wasn't going to say her name.

"She never appealed to me. You have to know that deep down." He stood up and walked over to my chair. He bent down in front of me. "Now. I've been waiting for months. Can we seal the deal?"

"You do know that this is a binding deal once it's sealed," I warned with a teasing grin.

"This is the best deal I've ever made." He leaned in, making good on his promise.

CHAPTER 10

The following morning, I awoke on cloud 9. Nothing was going to change the mood I was in.

At least, when I planted my feet on the floor, and even when I poured myself into those yoga pants that would fit Clara, I thought the day was going to be great.

"Did she call to say yoga was cancelled?" Iris had her nose pressed up against the Tranquility Spa door; the condensation from her breath appeared then disappeared. She shoved her rolled-up yoga mat in my arms. "Here. I'm going to go look around back."

Iris left me right in time for Lucy Drake to show up. You guessed it. Fancy yoga outfit and all, looking good, but she wasn't going to dampen my mood. I certainly wasn't going to tell her about me and Mac. She'd find out when she saw us out and about or maybe Mac would tell her.

Regardless, I could see now how silly I'd been, and I blamed any out of character moments on my crazy hormones. In fact, I was having my own personal summer at that moment.

"What's going on?" Lucy tugged on the door of the spa. She knocked. "Did you knock?"

"Of course, I knocked." I wanted so bad to just let myself bask in my happiness about me and Mac. I wanted to blurt out how we are back together, and I might even have thought about spending my life with him. Legally. But I didn't. "Iris went around back to see if the back door was open."

I knew all the buildings had back doors, but I never knew if anyone used them. My parents had boarded up the back entrance of the diner years ago.

"I'm calling her." Lucy pulled her cell phone from the waistband of her yoga pants and tapped the phone. Her long nails clicked along the screen before she put it up to her ear. "Peaches, honey, are we having yoga this morning?"

Her question was followed up with a lot of mmhmmm, alright, I see, and ummms. All of them drawn out in her Southern tone she liked to hum on the radio.

"Okay. I'll tell Bernadette and Iris." Lucy slid her glance over to the side of the building when we heard Iris coming back around. "Umkay," she said, then hung up the phone, sticking it back in her yoga pants.

"No class today, but she wants to talk to Bernadette." Lucy's eyes narrowed. "I wonder if this has anything to do with Simon Little's murder."

"Murder?" Iris rolled her eyes. "Bernie found him. He wasn't murdered."

"I know Bernie found him. I tried to get her to talk to me about it, but her lips buttoned up tighter than the collar on Preacher Don's shirt. But I'm willing to listen now that we don't have yoga." She put a hand on her hips and shifted her weight.

"Puhleeze." Iris flipped her head. "Bernie has too much to do besides gossip about what's going on." She took her yoga mat from me. "Which means, not having yoga is good, so you can get on your mail carrier route quicker."

"I... a... I..." Lucy Drake finally closed her mouth after she stammered to talk. She rolled back her shoulders and looked down her nose at me. "If you do decide to change *your* mind about talking to me about what you found yesterday morning, I'm more than willing to talk."

She twisted around and walked down the sidewalk.

"I can't believe you told her all that about Mac." I let out a long sigh, catching out of the corner of my eye the lights inside of Tranquility Spa coming on. "And 'my special surprise'?" My head tilted, and my brows rose. "You were taking it a bit too far with that big lie."

"Who said I'm lying?" She had a faint grin that told me she knew something, and she knew I hated secrets or surprises.

"You better tell me right now if something is going on," I demanded to know, only to be interrupted by Peaches, who popped open the door.

"Get in here." Her head took a quick look to the left and right before she opened the door fully for us to walk in. "I've got a problem."

"You look like you've got a problem." Iris really should keep her thoughts to herself, even though she was right.

Peaches's usual sunny disposition was drained from her face. I saw a bead of sweat gathered at her temple, which appeared to have its own little pulse today.

"Oh gosh." Iris had furrowed brows, and her eyes were full of concern. "This calls for something sweet." She gently touched Peaches's arm and headed back toward the door. "I'll be right back."

Peaches burst into tears as soon as the door closed.

"Honey, what's wrong?" I asked the young woman who appeared to be having a meltdown.

"I didn't know who to turn to." Her chest did that quick heaving up and down as she tried to get her breath. "I think the sheriff thinks I killed Simon."

"Why on earth do you think that?" Was Lucy right? Was I right? Dang, I was getting really good at this sleuthing.

"Well, the package I asked you to take back." She nodded and reached behind her on the counter to get a tissue from the box.

"The return to sender one." Inwardly, I groaned when I realized I'd forgotten to pick it up.

"Yeah. Well, I couldn't bear to let it sit here. Taunting me to open it. You know?" she asked, but really it was more of a statement than a question. I continued to nod and ignored Iris when she hurried back in with a cake box in her hand. "So, I took it to the post office and gave it to Monica."

"What did I miss?" Iris asked and took out her specialty sweet potato coffee cake.

My eyes swelled up and so did my pant size just looking at it. I tried to focus on Peaches, but my mouth watered at the sight and smell of the big piece of coffee cake Iris had put in front of me.

The drizzle of caramel icing on top looked like little rivers of brown sugar that oozed down the side.

"I really shouldn't." Peaches looked at the big piece of coffee cake. "I really have to watch what I eat, or I blow up like a big balloon."

"Really, you should." Iris pushed the plate closer across the counter to Peaches. "Especially if you're going to the big house because all you're going to get in there is tapioca pudding, and it's fake."

"Iris." I gasped, my mouth flying open.

"I'm teasing her." Iris snorted. "But really, you should."

Peaches found a glimmer of a smile under her tears, and after the first bite, her tears dried up. It was a good time for us to eat our cake and let what Peaches was saying sink in.

"So, when Angela found the package from me at the scene,

she came over to my house last night and asked me why I'd returned the package." She wiped her finger across the plate to scoop up the excess caramel icing before licking it off.

"Why would she think you did it?" I questioned, then added, "Unless you broke in to the post office and got it back."

"I did go back to the post office after I'd thought about what on earth could be inside of the package he sent because my mind started to get the better of me. So, I started drinking my bourbon." Peaches's story was getting worse by the minute. "But I didn't go to the gas station. At least, I don't think I did."

"Did you get into the post office?" I asked.

"I don't know. I can't remember. All I know is that I was drinking, and I woke up in the post office parking lot when Nick found me this morning." Peaches blinked a few times and looked away with a shameful face. "Of course, when Angela Hafley contacted him, he told her about my relationship with Simon and how on edge it's been the last couple of weeks."

By "on edge", did she mean all the threats she not only gave Simon but Sarah, his girlfriend?

"Why would you want him dead?" Iris asked a very important question.

"I didn't. That's why I need you two to look into it." Peaches looked between us before she settled her eyes on me.

"You mean her." Iris pointed to me. "I don't do anything but listen to what she's found out. And feed her sugar."

"Sugar is important." I nodded. "Very when my brain is going a million miles a minute. You weren't very nice to Simon or Sarah."

"Yeah." Iris gestured between me and her. "We were witness to you and Sarah when she was here trying to do yoga."

"And I did overhear you on the phone with Simon." I hated to add salt to the wound, but if Peaches needed a reason for why she was a suspect, then she had to know what we had seen.

Peaches went into a deep blank stare, and if I'd seen her do this before the whole Simon incident, I'd have thought she was diving into her Zen state. When I looked at her a little closer, I didn't see much of a difference.

"I didn't kill him. How would I have killed him?" she asked.

"I have no idea how he died. When I found him, I saw a bottle of empty bourbon, and I kicked an open and empty prescription bottle, but I don't know what it was." I wished I'd looked now. "He did say he was in pain, and he had a written prescription in his hand when I saw him at the doctor's office, but I didn't question it."

"Wait." Peaches put her hand up. "Did you say bourbon?"

"Yes, and I hate to say it, but I think it was the bourbon you drink." I started to backpedal. "Which doesn't mean you took him the bourbon. I mean, anyone would buy that bourbon."

"Anyone but Simon." A cloud of worry shadowed her face. "He doesn't drink alcohol often. He certainly doesn't drink bourbon since they can't claim it as gluten-free."

"Simon is gluten intolerant?" Iris sat up a little taller. "I understand gluten-free really well as a baker. Now that you mention it, I did make Simon's mother a gluten-free cake for his birthday last year."

"Which means he didn't drink bourbon. But who did?" I added that to my list of questions rolling around in my head and casually looked at Iris.

She was like a mind reader. She jumped up and grabbed one of Tranquility Spa's flyers with the monthly scheduled classes on it, flipped it over, and quickly started to write down the questions we were throwing out and possibilities of other suspects.

I knew once we were out of here, we'd turn the Pie in the Face kitchen into our investigation headquarters, where we used Iris's big whiteboard to list our suspects and their motives as to why they would've killed Simon.

"See..." Peaches looked under the counter and then around the counter before she buried her head into the trash. "I..." She gulped. "I can't find my bourbon."

I closed my eyes and sucked in a deep breath. As much as I didn't want to believe it, Peaches Partin was definitely Angela Hafley's number one suspect. And I was convinced that she didn't do it.

CHAPTER 11

"That's why we need to look into it," Iris demanded as we walked back to my house to discuss if we really were going to help out Peaches. We'd left when China had come to be with Peaches after Peaches had texted her. I felt comfortable leaving Peaches with her best friend and told China to call me if Peaches remembered anything else.

"I don't know." I shook my head and felt a little better with the sunrise on the horizon. Why was it that everything felt so much better with a little light? "You and I both heard her treat Sarah terribly. All because Sarah wanted to take yoga classes, and Tranquility Spa is the only place around here to do it."

"What about Nick?" Iris brought up another person I would look into. "You even mentioned how he was taken aback by the patent. He conveniently found Peaches?"

"We should be able to find out what Peaches did from the security cameras at the post office, which is why I think Angela believes Peaches killed him." I knew the first thing the sheriff or the FBI would do was get the postmaster general to give them access to the security footage. "There's nothing we can do that the FBI couldn't do better."

"FBI?" Iris jerked the gate to my house open.

"Breaking in to a post office is a federal crime, Iris. If Peaches did that and killed Simon, she's never going to get out of it no matter what." I unlocked the front door where we were greeted by a very happy Buster.

Iris melted down into the rocking chair as if the life had been sucked right out of her. Buster still brought out a smile on her face when he continued to jump up on her and give her some kisses.

"Hello!" Harriette Pearl was waddling down the sidewalk with her glass coffeepot in her hand. "I came down for a little coffee this morning."

"What's this about?" Iris asked.

"I see you two have been doing some exercise." Harriette eyeballed our outfits. "I made fresh coffee to get your day started."

"Spill it, Harriette." Iris slowly rocked back and forth in the rocking chair.

"Buster, down," I called out to Buster when he tried to jump on Harriette, who was already unstable. I met her on the front sidewalk and took the hot pot of coffee from her. "Wow, you brought the entire pot."

"Mmhhmmm," she ho-hummed, winking at me.

"Yeah, yeah. I know why you're here." I recalled the little curtain spying last night when Mac went to kiss me. "You interrupted a kiss."

"Oh Bernie, I'm so sorry. It was just when you and Mac started to get close, I couldn't contain my excitement and just plum squealed. I almost peed myself, which isn't unusual for my age, but still." She put her hand to her chest.

"Kissing? What kissing?" Iris leapt to her feet. "Who was kissing? I thought you came down here because you heard Simon Little was murdered."

"Murdered! Simon Little was murdered?" Harriette threw her hand over her mouth. "Oh, dear me."

"Yes. Mac and I kinda sorta got back together last night." I could tell by the changing expressions on Iris's face that she wasn't happy I'd not told her of it yet. "Seriously, I was going to tell you, but then this morning with Lucy happened, then the whole Peaches thing."

"What Peaches thing? Did she kill Simon?" Harriette's mind was churning so fast I could almost see the steam rolling out of her ears. "I did hear from Millie Barnes how his own mama was talking about Simon and his sickness, but to think Peaches murdered him. And Lucy"—Harriette's eyes lit up—"I hope she strained a muscle at yoga when you told her you and Mac were back together."

"First off, Peaches didn't kill Simon." Iris put her hand on her hips.

"You don't know that," I said.

"We need coffee." Harriette held on to the railing, went up the three steps to my house, and walked right on through the front screen door.

"I guess we are going to have coffee." I nudged Iris on my way past her.

"I guess you're gonna tell me what happened with Mac first." She shoved past me and picked up Rowena, who was sitting on the top of the chair just inside of the door. "The full story."

Buster bolted in before the screen door closed completely and skidded straight into the kitchen, afraid he wasn't going to get a treat he knew Iris would flip his way. And she did.

"Now, what's this business about Simon?" Harriette was seated at one of the chairs at the kitchen table, and Iris joined her after she gave the fur babies a few more treats.

"I want to hear about this kiss and Mac," Iris demanded

since I'd completely left out the Lucy Drake part in the story I'd shared with her before yoga.

"I couldn't help but look out the window last night and notice Mac had his romancing lights on in the back." Harriette had called Mac's twinkling lights on his back porch "romance lights" because she'd claimed he only had them on when I was over there for cookouts. "I was going to throw a fit if I saw him even touch that Lucy Drake. I mean a fit if even their toes touched under the table." She drew a deep breath in and relaxed a little more in the chair. "I kept an eye out too. He didn't even sit by her. Then they had a beer, but that didn't last long before Lucy took a phone call. That's when I raised all the windows on that side of my house because it was warm in my house, and the breeze at night just so happens to shoot right on that side of the house."

"Mmhmm, I bet it does." Iris's eyes lowered, mocking Harriette and her favorite excuse to use when she regurgitated the information to the Front Porch Ladies later.

"I couldn't help but hear what was going on. And I was only looking out for Bernie." Harriette was being too kind, and I meant too kind as in out of character.

Who was she trying to fool? Me or herself? She certainly wasn't pulling one over on Iris because Iris grunted and groaned with every lie coming out of the eighty-something-year-old's mouth.

"Then I saw Bernie hunkered down near my gate, and then I had to make sure I didn't need to come out there and have her back when Lucy saw her sneaking around to watch them."

"I was not sneaking around." I couldn't believe she said that. "Don't you be going around telling people I was checking up on Mac and who he was entertaining."

"I saw it with my own two eyes." Harriette pointed to her eyes. "I might be old, and things might not work one hundred percent like they used to, but my eyesight is really good." She folded her arms in front of her. "Ask Doc Adams."

Doctor Josh Adams was Sugar Creek Gap's eye doctor, and I wasn't going to call him up and ask him if Harriette Pearl had good eyesight or not. I was there, and I wasn't spying.

"I heard them walking around the corner as I was walking by, and I didn't want them to think I was spying on them, that's why I bent down." I only told the truth. "So, don't you even mention it to anyone or..."

Then I did it. I pulled my mail carrier card.

"I'll be late delivering your mail for a month," I threatened her.

"You wouldn't." She gasped.

"Try me." I confidently walked over to the cabinet to retrieve three coffee mugs and poured each one of us a big cup. "Now, let's get down to the real business." I sat a mug in front of each one of them. "Mac and I are going to try to make a go of this relationship thing. It's between me and him."

"And me," Iris mouthed so Harriette didn't hear her.

"What part of me saying I've got good eyesight did you not hear?" Harriette snarled at Iris. "I have good peripheral vision too."

"It's between me and Mac." I made myself clear again. "But I could use all the eyes, no matter how perfect they are, and ears on the ground when you hear someone say something about Simon Little or anything to do with him or people he knew."

Then it began like second nature. I'd made a plan before I had to get the two of them out of here so I could get ready for work and put the investigation into play. Iris was going to keep her eyes and ears peeled at the bakery since people would definitely go in there to purchase some baked goods to take to the family.

Harriette was going to make a casserole to take over to

Simon's mom's house, where she said she'd ask all sorts of questions. When I told her that was rude, she replied, *"Oh, they'll just say how I'm old and old people think they can just ask or say anything."*

That was true. Why did the older we get the more we thought our mouths could just spit whatever comes out or even give an opinion when one wasn't necessary? I remember when Richard had died and women in the community who were much older than me, including Harriette and all the Front Porch Ladies, just doled out advice like they were giving away free water. I didn't want to hear it, but I would stand there with a smile on my face, thinking exactly what Harriette said they'd say about her as she inquired at the Little's house when she dropped off her casserole.

With the plan set in motion, I knew I had to not only linger a little at the sheriff's department when I delivered their mail and picked Vita's brain, but also at the Sugar Creek Gap Funeral Home. There I could get some answers from either Barron Long, the actual elected coroner, or Jigs Baker, the owner of the funeral home, who assisted Barron since the morgue was located in the funeral home. Both places were my customers, and with the Wallflower on the way, I'd be sure to get something good Mom had made and sweeten up the conversation I wanted to have with them.

"Do we know anything yet about the break-in?" I asked Monica when I picked up the first and second loop of mail, which was not normal for me. Normally, I picked up one loop at a time, but today I was on a mission. And I couldn't help but have a giddyup in my step after I'd gotten an early morning text from Mac.

He only confirmed something special he'd planned for the evening, and it had to be the secret Iris was talking about. It did put a smile on my face.

"The authorities came in here and spent a lot of the day going through the camera footage. I know it did show someone, but they wouldn't say who." Monica looked over the LLV clipboards before she picked up the phone and dialed. "I've got a few vehicles that need to be looked at." She hung up.

"Was that Nick?" I asked.

"Yeah. He'll be right over." She ran her finger through her hair. "Do I look tired?"

"No." Was that a question she really wanted me to answer? That seemed like one of those questions that felt like a trick, or if I did tell her how I'd noticed she had much larger dark circles under her eyes, would she really want to hear that?

"Do I have enough lipstick on? You know, one can never have too much lipstick on." She swiped the tip of her finger at the corners of her mouth and repeated the statement that'd literally been beat into our heads as Southern young women.

"You look fine." Then it struck me. "Are you trying to impress Nick Kirby?"

"Noooooooo." Her lips formed an O, and her expression became even more vivid as she dragged the vowel out.

"Oh, my goodness." I couldn't help but smile. "You think he's cute."

"Bernadette Butler." She put her hands on her hips and thrust one hip to the side. "I'm not going to be your little project."

"Project?" I wasn't sure if I should take offense to that or not.

"I'm sorry. I guess I kinda felt like you were being my mom." She sighed.

"I'm not at all. I'm only Grady's mom, but I am a good person to run things by if you ever need me." I gave her a reassuring smile and remembered what it was like when I first admitted my feelings for Mac and how I did feel like a much younger version of myself. "Besides, I've never had a daughter, so I couldn't give you any dating advice, but I could give you advice on how boys think, and by boys, I mean men too."

"If that's the case, and if I were interested in Nick Kirby, how do I get him to notice me when he comes here so early in the morning?" she asked.

"Being yourself is enough." I knew she didn't want to hear that by the look on her face. "I know that is a mom thing to say, but you're amazing, and any man that is worth your time will see that, but there are ways to get him to talk more and get to know you."

"Go on. I'm listening." Her lips quivered as she tried to hide the big smile that curled up on the edges of her lips, but she finally gave in when her face blushed.

"Here." I dug down into the bag I'd brought from home and took out the box Iris had given me with my sweet treat for Vita. "I only need a couple of slices of this, so when Nick comes in, have a cup of coffee handy and offer this piece of strawberry shortcake to him." I held the box out. "Just take one slice because I need this to bribe Vita down at the sheriff's department."

It was no big secret to anyone in our small town how I was always sticking my nose into crimes and how I'd helped a few people get off Angela's suspect list, which was why Peaches had asked me to help.

"The first rule of thumb to get any man to talk and notice you is his stomach." I patted mine and couldn't help but think I might be getting a tad bit smaller. Just a smidgen, but it was better than nothing or getting bigger.

"I just brewed a fresh pot of coffee in the back too." Monica bounced on her toes and scurried back to what the post office considered the employee lounge.

It was a room with horrible lighting and a long fold-out table with plastic chairs along with a couple of old-style vending machines that had to have a few fist pounds to the glass to get the snack to fall.

"I brought you a cup too." She came back into the room with a plate under her arm and her hands filled with three coffees, carrying them in a triangular form.

"I put your stuff over there." She pointed to a different bag that was new and not broken in like my other one that was now held hostage by the sheriff's department.

"Thanks." Inwardly, I groaned when I picked it up and felt how stiff the strap was by pinching it in my fist. "Another few months and this will be broken in."

"Maybe if they can get the person on the camera in custody, you can get your old one back." Monica continued to sort through the large wheeled bins that were full of mail to be placed in the PO boxes.

"Do you know anything about the person?" I asked. I stuffed the Pie in the Face box in the new bag along with the duck pellets I'd also brought from home for my duck friend on Little Creek Road. "Like female or male?"

"No." She quickly shoved the envelopes in the correct slots. "They didn't say a word. Literally walked out of here stiff and tight-lipped. But I'm more than happy to report back to you today what they find or discuss when they come back."

"Was it just Angela here looking at the tapes?" I was curious to see who was here, so when I did deliver the mail at the sheriff's department, I'd know who might be in my back pocket.

"Vita and Angela were it." Monica glanced around the corner when the back door of the post office opened.

"Vita?" I made sure I heard her correctly, because Vita was my go-to gal, and I knew the strawberry shortcake was going to work.

"Good morning." Nick Kirby popped his head into the room. "I just wanted to let you know I'm here." His eyes went directly to the piece of cake. "Wow. I don't think I've ever seen you eating, Monica."

"I'm stuffed, but that's an extra piece if you'd like it. I also have a cup of coffee there too." Monica was a quick learner.

"Are you sure?" he asked, giving her a smile.

"I wouldn't've offered it to you if I weren't." Her shoulders swayed back and forth.

"That didn't take long." I had to break the awkward moment. Though I didn't discourage Monica away from him since I wasn't one-hundred-percent positive he had something to do with Simon's murder, but I did put an eye on him. Nick was on my very short list of suspects.

"I was just over at the Roasted Bean grabbing a cup of coffee before I headed on over." He grabbed the work orders from the file that hung on the wall. "But I sure could use more." He sat down in the folding chair and put the file on the table, flipping through the orders from the LLV mail carriers. "Looks easy this morning." He quickly looked through them while sipping his coffee from Monica.

By Monica's reaction, I could tell she had more than a crush on him, she truly liked him and wanted him to return the favor, like, today.

"What's your deal?" Monica asked after Nick left to go work on the LLVs and I threw a couple of questions at him.

"I just don't like a stiff strap." I shrugged and placed the new bag across my body. "Makes for an uncomfortable day."

"I'm sorry about that." Monica continued to toss the mail into the PO box slots. "Maybe you can throw it into the wash tonight."

"Yeah. Good idea." I waved goodbye to her on my way out of the door with my eyes set on Nick.

He was right where I wanted him. In the parking lot with other mail carriers walking around. On my way over to the vehicle he was working on, I overheard a few of my colleagues talking about Simon and how they'd also heard it was murder.

"How are you doing?" I asked Nick.

"I'm good. You?" He was fiddling with some hoses on the vehicle.

"I'm fine. But I really wanted to make sure you're okay," I said with sympathy laced in my tone. "I know it's got to be hard losing your best friend and business partner."

"Yeah." He let go of the hoses and stood up. "Honestly, I don't think it's hit me yet. I just have a hard time wrapping my head around Peaches doing such a thing to him. And breaking in to the post office." He shook his head with disbelief written all over his face.

Very convincingly, I might add.

"I knew she was a drinker and Simon hated that about her, which is why he broke up with her. She accused him of all sorts of things last week when she showed up at the garage, throwing a big hissy fit." Nick was telling me some information that I didn't even have to pull from him. A grunting noise escaped him, like he was about to say something, but didn't. "But that's for the sheriff to sort out. I'm just going to try to honor him by doing what he wanted, and that's to get that motorcycle patent done."

"You mean the patent he'd filed, and I tried to deliver?" I questioned.

"Yeah. I called the patent office, and I have all the paperwork to refile under my name. I told Simon's mom I was going to be sure to give them half the money of everything we sell with it since Simon was half of it."

"That's kind of you." *Of course it's kind of you, you murderer.* I tried to stop my thinking, but the more I looked at him and listened to him talk, it was clear he wasn't happy that Simon filed the patent without him. Or at least I could only think he'd filed it without him since the certified letter was only for Simon to sign. "What was the part anyways?"

It was something I'd talked about in passing with Simon that day in the doctor's office, but I really wanted to be clear on the exact part so I could see if it was really worth killing over.

"I didn't know you were interested in motorcycles." He threw a stare at me, making it seem as though he wasn't going to make this little snooping thing easy.

"I care about Simon, and you know, my curiosity was up when I was delivering it. Very interesting piece of mail when nothing ever happens around here." Who was I kidding? Sugar Creek Gap had a lot going on with a few murders over the last couple of years, but it was all for the sake of trying to figure out if Peaches was telling the truth that she didn't kill Simon, or if Nick was telling me the truth about Peaches.

"Actually," he said, taking a few steps toward me. There was excitement building in his voice with each word. Using his hands, he explained, "It's pretty cool. We'd gotten a few bikes in the shop with the same malfunctions, specifically the separation and crimping failure in the front upper stanchions."

"The what?" I had no clue what he was talking about or trying to show me with his arm.

"There's a fork in the front suspension of the bike." He wasn't explaining what it was fully but just enough that I knew where the handlebars of motorcycle were located. "For some reason, these things come loose and don't stay clamped. It's pretty crazy how these are not made properly and people have to keep replacing them. Simon came up with an amazing idea to make a clamp. He sold me when his eyes lit up about how we could sell them. I came up with a prototype, and we tried it out. It took months but we finally came up with one that worked on the bikes we repaired."

It was all fascinating really. Nick. Gosh, he lit up so bright as he talked about it, reminding me of how Simon had gotten excited in the doctor's office when I told him about the letter.

"Yeah. I mean, cool, right?" Nick smiled. Then I watched it falter as he continued, "Simon was good at the business stuff while I did most of the hands-on stuff, which would make it hard to continue keeping the garage open."

"What about the patent?" I asked.

"I have enough of the paperwork to show that I put the parts together to make it while Simon came up with the actual idea, so it's enough for me to refile and get the thing into production. I just wish he was here to see it all come together." Nick shuffled a small rock underneath his shoe.

"About that. Do you know anyone who would want the letter so bad that they'd break in to the post office?" I wanted to bring it back around to shed light on him as a suspect.

"Like I told Angela, when I found Peaches here, I had no idea she'd broke in to the post office. She was passed out cold. I took her back to her exercise place and left her there. I came back and found Monica here. She'd already called the police. But I know Peaches didn't want Simon to succeed in anything." Nick ran a dirty hand through his hair, making it stick up all over the place. "Like I said, when she came by the garage the other day, she was hootin' and hollerin' about how he was sending Sarah into the studio to make her jealous and she didn't care if he did have his surgery and wished his patent didn't go through. It was crazy train."

"That seems so out of her character." I'd never seen Peaches as a drinker or having anger issues. "She's the calmest person I'd ever seen."

"Well, turnip tops don't tell you the size of the turnip either." It was our way of saying that you can't judge a book by its cover.

"I guess not." His story bothered me more than I wanted it to. I really liked Peaches, but if what he was saying was true, it was her that I needed to look into, and I certainly couldn't help a killer out as she'd asked. "I just can't believe it."

"Don't believe me. Ask Sarah Hodge. That is one classy lady. She never said a foul word about Peaches the entire time Peaches threatened her. All Sarah would say to Simon was that Peaches was sick and she couldn't help it."

I wasn't buying the whole Sarah-Hodges-wasn't-a-victim act. I'd seen her and Peaches go at it at Tranquility Spa, and Sarah was no fly on the wall.

There was one thing I did know. I needed Harriette Pearl to ask some questions today on her little visit to the Little's home. And giving her a call on my way over to the Sugar Creek Nursing Home was a current priority.

"Harriette, it's Bernie." I apologized because her voice cracked when she answered like I'd woken her up. "I'm sorry. Did I wake you?" I questioned, thinking it was odd she'd gone back to bed after I'd just seen her a little while ago.

"What's wrong?" Her quiet voice turned to alarm. "Are you okay? Do I need to get my gun?"

"Lord no." The last thing Sugar Creek Gap needed was Harriette Pearl taking her gun anywhere. "I need you to ask Simon's mom about the patent Simon had filed for the motorcycle riser."

"Motorcycle what?" Harriette was confused, so I needed to make it simpler.

"You know the patent letter I'd told you about and how I'd tried to deliver it and Nick Kirby seemed interested. Too interested?"

"Really?" Her Southern drawl oozed through the phone

along with her curiosity. "I'll definitely throw that into the conversation when I visit with his mama. I'll keep you posted."

"Go back to bed." I realized she probably went back to sleep after she left my house since it was early.

"Don't be going and telling people I was sleeping this late. I was resting my eyes," she corrected me.

CHAPTER 12

The morning delivery at the Sugar Creek Nursing Home went smooth as usual and much quicker since I was hustling to get to Tranquility to check on Peaches. I was going to find out if she really had this drinking problem Nick had referred to several times when I'd seen him this morning at the post office.

The sign on the Tranquility Wellness was flipped open, which gave me a little reassurance Peaches had cleaned herself up this morning to get on with her day, though I knew it was going to be tough.

"Any mail today?" I asked Peaches when I noticed she was hanging up some of the clothing items she had for sale.

"I didn't see any." China whirled around. "Hey, Bernie. Thanks so much for this morning. Peaches is a mess of monkeys, and I told her she needed to get in to see Doc Hunter before this thing spirals out of control."

"What thing?" I asked and put the rubber-banded bundle of incoming mail in the basket on the counter.

"Let's be honest." China walked over and folded a yoga shirt, placing it neatly on top of the counter. "I know you've helped out a few times in these murder cases. If what Peaches says is true about her going to the post office, and Angela finding that bourbon bottle at the gas station, then this doesn't look good."

"I didn't want to tell her that this morning, but after she asked for my help, it was her way of telling me she already knew she was a suspect."

China's eyes bolted open in surprise.

"She is?" She gasped, pulling her lips together as her eyes welled with a line of tears. "I'm sorry." She shook her head and then her hands before she grabbed a tissue from the box. "I've been telling her for the past three months that she needed to get help for her drinking. I told her this wasn't going to end well and now..." Her voice cracked. "I could've stopped this if I'd only done what her mom had asked me to do."

"What was that?" I just couldn't believe I was hearing this. Peaches was the last person I ever thought would have a drinking issue.

"I had a meeting here for my clothing line that Peaches had encouraged me to make, which reminds me that I've got your shirt." China had a range of emotions cross her face. Sadness was the first one I noticed as she talked about Peaches. The love she had for her best friend was apparent. Then her sadness turned to pride as she spoke about her line of yoga clothes. "The meeting was here; in fact, all our meetings have been here, and she's never completed one."

"What does that have to do with her mom?" I wondered and recalled how just the other day Peaches wasn't able to talk to China after she'd kicked Sarah Hodges out of Tranquility Wellness's yoga class.

"I was talking to her mom over at the bank, and she asked if anyone had bought any of my clothes here in the retail area.

When I told her Peaches and I hadn't really discussed it, she mentioned how worried the family was because Peaches hadn't been over for Sunday supper, and the last time she did come, she drank too much and had to be driven home." China's lips turned down. "Then there was the time she blacked out."

"Like she did at the post office? Where she didn't remember anything?" I asked because this certainly wasn't going to help Peaches's case any. Especially if she had a history of this type of behavior.

"Yes. And her mother sent Tim Crouse down to the department to see if Peaches was a suspect this morning after Lucy Drake had reported Simon's death had been ruled as suspicious. That's when they came down here and got her. Which is why I'm here. I told them I'd keep the retail shop open so Peaches can have money coming in while she takes time off."

"Time off?" There'd been so much that'd happened with Peaches that I wasn't able to keep up with everything.

"Oh yeah. Her mom took her to an AA meeting at the Sugar Creek Baptist Church and..." There was a bit of an uncomfortable pause as if China didn't want to tell me.

"You can tell me. This morning before you got here, when Iris and I were here, Peaches asked me to help her because she knew she was possibly going to be a suspect." And when I said that out loud, it made it sound as though Peaches needed to get things in place like a real suspect would do.

I'd seen it in all the crime shows where the criminal would be sure to plant various things to take the sleuth off their trail, and I couldn't help wondering if that was something Peaches would do. It was definitely not in her nature, but anything Peaches was doing now wasn't like the Peaches I knew.

"Is she really an alcoholic, or does she just drink a little too much?" There were clearly things I needed to know since I'd sort of agreed to look into things.

"Peaches hasn't always been this relaxed." China's hands swept in front of her as though she were showcasing the place. "Before she got her yoga hours to be a teacher, she was actually pretty wild growing up. It wasn't until her parents had sent her to Florida to visit family that she came back changed. Simon loved it. It was like they fell in love all over again, but this time it was so respectful."

"When did she start drinking again?" I needed to know what threw Peaches back to the brink of wanting to go back or if it was simply just the addiction.

"Tranquility Wellness is on the brink of closing." Her brows dipped as she frowned. "I really have been trying to help her with my clothing line. It was going to be another stream of income to help pay the bills." Her mouth widened in a dramatic O as her eyes grew wide. "Which reminds me to give you your shirt." She held a finger up and disappeared into the hallway with the Reiki rooms.

I walked around, trying to remember how excited Peaches was when I first met her. I'd heard of her parents, though I'd never met them. Even though Sugar Creek Gap was small, the outskirts of town had really grown. It felt like we went from five thousand citizens to twelve thousand overnight.

Peaches had bounced on the balls of her feet with excitement as she told me all her plans and had invited me for free classes. I didn't take advantage of those, and now my muscles told me why.

"Here you go." China dangled a bag in front of her as she walked toward me. "You okay?"

"Yeah. I'm, well, I'm so sad this happened to Simon, Peaches, and now the shop." I pushed back anything else since I was sure China didn't care about me rambling. I pulled the shirt out. "Thanks. This is great."

"You're going to love the material when you're practicing."

She abruptly stopped. Her eyes filled with tears. "I'm sorry." She gulped. "I'm trying to be strong for Peaches, but seeing her dream come crashing down around her while she's being accused of murder is killing me."

"I'm so sorry." I gave her a warm hug. "I know how hard it is to see your best friend go through something you can't help them with. I know me and Iris are old, but when we were a little older than you, Iris went through a divorce, and I spent many days trying to help her. Then, she was there for me when my husband died."

I shook my head to stop my mouth from rambling.

"What I'm saying is that you really don't have to do anything but just be there for her. Sometimes I didn't want to talk about what was happening, so Iris would just sit with me, and we didn't talk. Or we'd just eat." I patted my stomach. "Which you can see we still do."

That made China laugh, and it was my cue to leave.

"Y'all are going to be okay." I assured her on my way out the door, even though I didn't believe it myself.

Even dropping off my parents' mail at the Wallflower Diner and Mac's mail at his office didn't help me get Peaches out of my head. Which was why I didn't dillydally getting down to the sheriff's department.

"Morning, Bernie!" Vita Dickens hollered from her much-deserved desk. Her shiny new deputy sheriff's pin was brighter than the sun.

"Look at you all official," I joked and handed the mail to the new dispatcher who'd taken Vita's place. "I'm glad you're here. I got you a little something."

I dug down into my bag and got the strawberry shortcake Iris had given me for my little bribery treat.

"Bernadette, if I didn't know better, I'd think you were trying to get some information out of me." Vita said.

"Vita, now why would I try to bribe the eyes and ears of the department when I found a person who was dead, and now I found out through the grapevine, he'd actually been murdered?" I could see from the glint in her eye that she knew darn well why I was there. "I'm not going to sugarcoat it with this delicious strawberry treat." I opened the box and waved it under her nose. "But I do recall strawberry anything is your fav."

"You are the devil, Bernadette Butler." She grabbed the box and motioned for me to sit down. She reached to the farthest corner of her desk, retrieving a file. "I'm not sure what you heard"—she put air quotes on the word "heard"—"but while you keep me company"—she took the plastic fork and snagged a big piece of the cake—"I'll tell you what we know since I know you're not going to stop snooping," she mumbled after she put the forkful in her mouth.

"Oh Vita, you know me well." I took a breath and looked around. "Angela not here?"

"Nope." She opened the file and flipped it around. "As you can see, Simon Little didn't have an ounce of bourbon in his system. He had a belly full of sports drink with a nice little mixture of sleeping pills. Only..." She took another bite and moved her finger to the file where they'd gotten Doctor Hunter's patient notes documented. "Doc Hunter has never given him a prescription for sleeping pills or pain pills."

"There you are."

I jumped, cursing under my breath as Sheriff Angela Hafley came up behind me.

"Oh, settle down." She looked at me and motioned for me to sit back down. "We know you by now and figured you'd be in here once you heard Simon was murdered. I told Vita to keep an eye out for you." She lifted her chin. "Nothing for me? I like sweets."

"I-I...um..." I stammered for words, unsure of what was going on. "I can bring you some tomorrow."

"I'm teasing." She reached in front of me and took the file. "I'll take it from here, Vita. You enjoy that cake while I take Bernadette back into the interrogation room." She waved the folder for me to follow her.

Vita shrugged and stuffed another big bite in her mouth when I got up and walked by her with big eyes, trying to tell her that I knew she'd set me up this whole time, making me believe I had bribed her. Darn Vita.

"What all did Vita tell you?" Angela had me sit across from her once we made it into the small room with the large glass window where others could watch and listen to what was going on at any given moment.

"She just finished telling me how he didn't have bourbon in his system and the doctor never prescribed him pills." I left it to a minimum. My eyes adjusted to the low lighting in the room. They sure did need a remodel to the old department.

"Did she tell you that there was bourbon in his mouth?" She opened the file and shoved it across the table to me.

"No." My head jerked up. My jaw dropped, then the shock set in. "Are you telling me that someone had put the bourbon in his mouth after he was dead?"

"I think someone he knew was with him. There was no struggle. I believe his medication for his hands were on his desk. Someone came in. I think he left the room, and someone slipped a bunch of pills into the dark purple sports drink. The note on the computer written by him"—she put "him" in air quotes—"said he took the pills and downed the full bottle of bourbon to make sure it done the trick. There was no bourbon in his stomach."

She stood up and walked over to the small table in the

corner with various bagged items on top of it. I realized it was all the evidence from the scene.

"You can see a little sediment in the bottom." She held up the bag with the practically empty sports drink. "We did a few experiments today. We crushed up the number of sleeping pills it would take to kill Simon per his height and weight. We got the same purple sports drink, and if the pills were crushed very fine, it would be impossible for him to see unless he held it up to look into it." She put the evidence bag back on the table. "Why would he do that if he trusted the person he was with?"

"What about the pill bottle I kicked when I found him?" I wanted to know who that belonged to.

"It was his medication. Empty. So that makes me think the killer set the scene after he passed out, then stopped breathing." Angela reached over the table and pointed to the area where she'd started to recreate the scene.

"You think the killer had the pills already crushed and knew he drank the sports drink. Or maybe brought the bourbon, which he doesn't drink, for them to have together." I recalled Peaches telling me about Simon being gluten intolerant. "And he's allergic to gluten." It looked like I'd about knocked her over with a feather. "What? You didn't know?"

"No. Which means Peaches Partin might not be his killer."

"Why do you think she'd kill him?" I asked. "She dated him for a long time, and she'd know if he was gluten intolerant. It's not just some alcohol; it can be food too. They were very serious from what Peaches had told me. So, whoever killed Simon didn't know he was gluten intolerant because he'd never drink it. And it's one reason why he and Peaches broke up."

"His gluten-free diet?" Angela questioned.

"No. Her drinking because he didn't drink." I told her about Peaches and her history.

"Peaches should be here in an hour or so with Tim Crouse."

Angela was no different than most law enforcement officers when it came to the idea that when suspects lawyered up, they were hiding something.

But I believed, in this case, Peaches knew, and she'd said it earlier that she felt she was the suspect since her fingerprints were all over the place.

"Only Peaches's prints were on the bottle?" I asked.

"There weren't any prints on the bottle." Angela's brows rose. "The only prints we found besides Nick's and Simon's were on the post office box, and those were Peaches."

"The return to sender box." I groaned and felt my shoulders fall. "I was supposed to pick that up from her at her shop, and I completely forgot. Now I'm upset that she did go back to the post office and—" I abruptly stopped talking.

Nick Kirby popped into my head.

His prints were all over since he also worked there. I couldn't help but recall the look on his face when I was holding the certified letter for Simon.

"What are you thinking?" Angela reached across the table and took the file back, closing it.

"I'm wondering if you're going to ask me to be a consultant again." I was getting good at making things up on the fly.

My true answer would've been that I was thinking Nick Kirby was the killer and had the most motive, plus he was at the post office and took Peaches back to Tranquility Wellness. Mmhhmm... how convenient.

"I do think it went well last time, though I didn't like how you put yourself in danger in the end, so this time I think we should have more open communication where you just send me the little tidbits as you get them." It was her way of telling me that she didn't like how I kept the clues I'd heard close to the cuff and gave them to her all at once.

"No problem," I agreed and used my hands on the table to

push up to standing. "I must be getting the rest of the mail delivered." I hoisted my bag up on my shoulder and made sure the strap band was securely in place and perfectly resting on my shoulder muscle so it was comfortable for the walk to the garage.

Nick Kirby was next on my list.

CHAPTER 13

The sun's glow touched down into my soul. The closer I got to the garage, the warmer I felt about getting to the heart of Simon Little's death and who killed him.

Images of his face when he talked about the Dupuytren's contracture made my heart ache, but as soon as he mentioned the motorcycle part he'd patented and intended to make, it put a sense of ease into his body language.

His audible sigh of relief as he told me about how it would help pay for his surgery, and how he'd planned to get back to work on the cars in the garage along with Nick, played out in my head like the breeze as it swept across the tall grass in the fields between the garage and the funeral home.

That gentle rustling of the grass was replaced with the sounds of arguing between a man and a woman.

Not that I was trying to tiptoe upon anyone, though I might've used that technique, but I wanted to get close enough so I could see exactly who and what they were fussing about.

Instead of going into the open garage door, I crept along the side of the building and around so I could be on the outside wall. I knew Nick's voice as the male. The woman's voice was vaguely familiar, but I was unable to recall who it might be.

I put both hands on the strap of the mailbag, not only to steady the bag from going forward when I bent down and leaned in to listen, but also to steady myself from falling over and keep my hands from shaking.

Deep breath in, I thought, repeating what Peaches was teaching us in class. If the promises of Doctor Hunter about yoga and stress relief going hand in hand were true, right now I was counting on that breath to help me stay calm, cool, and collected.

"I told you the sheriff came to my house today." The woman's shaky voice matched the manic pacing she was doing. "I got behind the couch and hid. Do you know I didn't answer the door because they were going to question me? I told you this whole thing was no good, but you couldn't stop yourself."

"I told you it is for our future, our life. And you had no problem slipping me the final plans." I could see the smirk on Nick's face as he responded to the woman, whose back was to me. "We knew that if we got caught, we'd have to pay the consequences."

Consequences? I gulped and closed my eyes, easing back around the corner of the garage. I slid down the wall and sat on the hot blacktop as I tried to catch my breath and figure out what exactly I needed to do.

No doubt in my mind that they were talking about Simon.

"You had no issue with this when he was alive. Now that he's dead, we can move forward with no one and nothing in the way. You're going to have to put on a brave face as the grieving girlfriend." Nick had no problem calling attention to the woman's weakness.

"Girlfriend?" I curled my lips together when I realized I'd whispered out loud.

Put on a brave face as the grieving girlfriend. My eyes shot open. I pulled the strap over my head and took the bag off to set it up against the wall. On hands and knees, I crawled back to the corner and, carefully, slowly, eased around to let one eyeball get a look to see if it was Sarah Hodge.

Nick stepped out of the way and moved toward the front of the garage, leaving room for her to turn around.

"Sarah." My heart fell into my hands and knees when I jerked back around the corner, resting my back against the wall as the worry started to go straight to my head. I could feel the stress crawl up my jaw, making it tense, before the tense feeling slithered up to the wrinkles on my forehead where it would settle. Soon, I'd get a big fat headache.

Deep breaths, deep breaths, I continued to repeat the mantra that was not helping and took deep breaths in my mouth, then out my nose, before I realized I wasn't doing it right. Then I switched it to breathe in the nose and out the mouth.

"Bernadette?" I heard someone call my name out. "Are you okay? Do I need to call the life squad?"

"Oh! Nick!" I gulped. "Sarah." My eyes shot open when I saw both of them staring down at me, their bodies in shadow from the sun.

"You're sweating." Sarah stepped a little closer, coming into view. "Nick, this isn't good. She does this in yoga, and I swear the woman is going to have a heart attack. Are you having a heart attack?" she asked me in quite a loud voice.

"She's not deaf." Nick bent down and got in my face. "Are you okay?"

"I'm fine." I waved them off and moved because they were sucking up all the air I needed to process the fact that I heard they killed Simon.

Maybe they didn't say that, but they sure did do something

awful that had to do with him. And what was more awful than killing him?

"I'm having a hot flash." I pushed myself up onto my feet and felt Nick's hand grab underneath my arm to help me. "Don't touch me," I snapped at him and grabbed my mail carrier bag, hoisting it back over my shoulder.

Was there any sort of weapon I could use in my bag? I tried to think of anything. Nothing. Just rubber bands around stacks of mail, which I guess I could shoot them off my finger if it came down to needing something as self-defense. Not that it would seriously hurt them, but they did sting when they hit the skin.

"Whoa!" He threw his hands up in the air.

"She's in menopause, and women don't like to be touched during menopause," Sarah spouted off like she knew what menopause was in her late twenty-something-year-old body.

"Let's get this straight." I shook a finger at both of them. "I'm fine. I was delivering the mail and decided to take a break. This wall looked like a good spot for a snack." I dug into my mail carrier bag to grab anything I had in there to eat. If I could pretend the lie was true, maybe they'd believe me and not realize I'd heard all the horrible details of their conversation.

"Are those duck pellets?" Sarah's nose curled when she noticed the bag I'd taken out. I'd stuffed a handful into my mouth.

"No." I shook my head and tried not to gag at the awful duck pellets. "It's a new form of protein and magnesium for leg and joint health since I walk so much."

The saliva in my mouth was sparse. I tried and tried to gulp the stuff down.

"Let me get you a water." Sarah hurried back around the building.

"Where's Gerome today?" Nick asked.

"He's off." I gripped my strap with both hands and took a few steps sideways, figuring I could take off running to the back of the building if it came down to that.

"Where is it?" Nick asked.

"Where's what?" I questioned him and looked at the cup in Sarah's hand as she came around the corner.

"My mail." He tilted his head and paused, giving me a questioning look.

"Here. Drink this." Sarah shoved the cup of water toward me. "She's probably not thinking clearly with the menopause." She tried to whisper it to him, but I clearly heard her.

"I'm not drinking your poison." I smacked the cup out of her hand just as Gerome in his LLV drove right on up.

"I thought you said Gerome was off." Nick's observation caused my chest to tighten, my muscles to tense, and my feet to feel like lead when I bolted around them with all the energy I had in me to get to Gerome.

"I'm so glad you're here," I gushed and grabbed Gerome's arm where his hands were still gripped on the wheel of his mail carrier truck.

"Hey, man." Nick gave a solid chin nod to Gerome. "I think something is wrong with her."

I noticed Gerome had given me a once-over.

"There's nothing wrong with me. You're the killer." I started to spit out accusations on how I heard them talking and how they had Simon out of the way. "Be the good grieving girlfriend," I said in a snide and condescending way.

Nick and Sarah stood there with their mouths gaping open, not saying a word, like they were in shock. I'd figured them out. Before I could get it all out, the postmaster had pulled up in his car, dragging me back to the post office.

CHAPTER 14

"Suspension?" My mom hurried around the counter of the Wallflower Diner, where I'd gone to get some sort of comfort food. "Bernie, what on earth did you do?" She eased down onto the stool next to me and put her arms around me.

I needed this more than food. I started to cry. A fifty-year-old woman crying on her mother's shoulder. I was pitiful.

"Lost my mind." I shook my head when I replayed all the crazy I'd hung out to dry right there on the gas station property.

"I'm going to get you an appointment with Doctor Hunter right now," she insisted before giving me one more bear hug sealed with a kiss on the top of my head. "Barry, you get her a cup of coffee!" she hollered down the counter to my dad.

My dad leaned over from his stool and looked down the counter.

"I'm fine, dad." I gave a slight wave before I wiped the tears off my cheeks.

My assuring him I was fine wasn't enough. His eyes narrowed and he stood up, walking down with a stalking movement.

"I'm gonna take care of that boy once and for all." He tugged on the suspenders clipped on his jeans and hoisted them up more around his thick waist. "Barbara, I'll be right back."

"Where are you going? Who are you taking care of?" I questioned.

"Mac Tabor. I heard you two were back together, and I loved that boy like my own until he started going out on you with Lucy Drake. Now that I see you in this state, it just gives me a reason to do what I need to do to that boy." My dad wrung a fist in the palm of his hand.

"Dad, first off, I'd like to see you fistfight with anyone at your age. Secondly, it's not Mac." I patted the empty stool next to me.

"Menopause." My mom had no shame as she hollered it out the kitchen pass-through.

"Oh." His facial features softened. "In that case, I'll let you talk to your mother."

"Coffee! Get her coffee!" Mom screamed the direction at him.

He did exactly like she told him to do, and I thanked him just as she put down a biscuit smothered in chocolate gravy in front of me.

"This calls for two biscuits before you get on down to your appointment with Doctor Hunter." Mom took a fork and took her own bite off my plate. "I'm a good cook."

"Yes, you are." I couldn't help but take a big bite myself. "But I don't have an appointment with Doctor Hunter."

"Yes, you do. I called in my favor when you were discussing with your dad." She had a way with words.

"Barbara, is this your daughter?" A woman with short dark hair approached us. She had on nice pale-yellow linen suit with a white lily pinned on the lapel.

"Corine, this is my Bernadette. Why don't you sit down and let me get you something?" Mom flung the towel off her shoulder and waved at me to move, gesturing for the woman to sit down in my spot like I was ten years old.

"Honey, you stay right there. I can't thank you enough for the friendship you've given Peaches. Her daddy and I are beside ourselves with everything going on, but she insists you're helping her." The woman's eyes were riddled with sadness, and that's when I recognized Peaches had her mother's eyes.

"Can't I get you something?" my mom insisted.

"I've got a to-go order already called in." she told Mom.

"Let me go check on it then." Mom hurried right back to the kitchen where I had no doubt she'd emerge victoriously with the order in her possession.

"I stopped by Peaches's shop, but China said Peaches had taken the day off." I lied again. Boy, I was going to have to say extra prayers of forgiveness tonight from all the falsehoods I've been spreading around like sprinkles on a cake.

"We just got out of our meeting with Tim Crouse before he took her down to the sheriff's department, where that awful woman sheriff is going to keep asking Peaches the same questions over and over again." Corine did finally sit down on the open stool next to me.

In a whip of an eye, my dad had poured her a cup of coffee and topped mine off.

"Thank you." Her Southern sweetness poured out of her mouth, and it reminded me of Peaches. The Peaches I knew, not the number one murder suspect.

"I really hope things get cleared up, and the real killer is caught." I considered the idea of telling her what I'd heard at the gas station, but as rumors spread around the town, I wasn't sure if she'd already heard. So, I kept my mouth shut.

"We are desperate for people to come forward with any information. My sweet Peaches has taken to the bottle again over this boy, and she just doesn't remember her whereabouts or going to the post office." Her lashes rapidly opened and closed with each blink. Stress deepened her crow's feet.

"I have a quick question." There I was, back in the middle of things when I should just leave well enough alone now that I was on suspension from my job. "Did you know Simon well?"

She drew back with a curious look.

"I did. Or at least I thought I did," she said.

"What about his relationship with Nick Kirby?" I asked.

"His business partner?" she asked for confirmation.

"Yes." I picked up my cup and took a sip so it appeared as casual conversation.

"I think they were good friends. He stopped by the house to see if Peaches was okay after he found out what happened to Simon."

"Don't you think that's odd that he'd stop by to check on Peaches? I mean, it does seem odd since she and Simon weren't dating. In fact, they didn't even like each other from what Peaches had told me." Nothing Nick was doing made sense.

"He and Peaches were always close, even after Simon broke it off with her. Nick had stopped by Peaches's apartment to check on her since he knew she'd started drinking again." Corine slowly shook her head. "I'm still not sure why she started to drink."

"Maybe her business. I mean, when you're financially in trouble, it's a lot of added stress." I noticed her visibly tense up when I mentioned how I'd heard about Tranquility Wellness having some money issues. Then I wanted to offer her some hope, so I continued, "Look at me. I just got put on suspension from the post office, and I really want a drink."

"Dear." She laid a flat palm on my back. "I'm so sorry. I would offer some sort of help, but I fear I'm in no shape to give anyone anything. Not even my own daughter."

"I'm fine." I assured her and got off the subject of money. "Where is Peaches staying?"

"She's staying with us until we can get this mess cleared up. I'm picking up food now to give me some time before I need to pick her up at the department." She bit the edge of her lip. "I do hope they don't arrest her."

"Me too." I wasn't sure, but I didn't think they could arrest her on what they had, though I'm sure people have been arrested with much less evidence against them. "I'd like to stop by and see her. Talk to her now that I have some free time to help on my hands."

"She'd love that. I'd love that. She says that you're the only one who can help her." Corine's attention turned to my mom and the to-go bags Mom set in front of her.

"It's on the house," Mom told her in a matter-of-fact, don't-try-to-argue-with-me way.

"You and your family are a blessing, Barbara." Corine reached out and grabbed my mom's hand. There was some sort of bond there I was unaware of. She let go and reached into her bag where she pulled out a pen and piece of paper, scribbling down their address. "You can stop by anytime this afternoon."

"Thank you, I will." I slipped the piece of paper into the pocket of my blue mail carrier uniform shorts. We said our goodbyes.

"I feel bad for her." My mom shook her head. "You and I both know what it's like to do anything for your child."

"Yes, we do," I whispered and watched Corine leave the diner before I turned back around to finish the biscuits and chocolate gravy. "How do you know her?"

"Elks club." Mom nodded, then headed down the counter to help another customer, who'd just sat down.

Mom left me alone to finish the food while she walked around the diner and greeted customers, asking if their food was good and about the service they were receiving. Mom ran a tight ship, but fair, and every one of her employees loved to work for her.

"You better get off now. You can't be late since I called in my favor." She took my plate and my coffee cup.

"What favor?" I asked, but she moved on down the line, ignoring me. "What favor?" I asked my dad.

He laughed and gave me a hug goodbye, not saying a word.

It was well past noon, and for a second, I wondered if I had enough time to run home and change before my appointment. I'd also thought about skipping this appointment since I had no idea why I was going. I guessed, even at fifty years old, you still tried to please your parents.

My phone chirped, and it was a text from Monica. She said the postmaster had given her my route for the next two weeks and wanted to make sure I was cool with that. Of course I wasn't, but I was going to embrace it in hopes this whole messy murder thing was cleared up by then.

Instead, I texted back, asking if she knew what the sheriff's department and FBI had found out from the cameras.

The text turned into a call.

"Too much to text. Besides, I wanted to make sure you're okay." Monica was sweet. She loved working the counter but had visions of getting a route of her own.

The counter could be stressful most days. The customers would get angry about waiting in line. Then the customers would come in wanting to know why they didn't get a package. Or they'd come in and complain about a package being destroyed in transit when the package was probably in shambles from the journey it'd taken.

"I'm fine. I guess I did too much snooping." I knew she already knew about my lofty ambitions when it came to crime around Sugar Creek Gap, and she was the first to jump on the bandwagon of helping me. "So, by you calling, I'm assuming you have some information."

"Peaches is clearly on the footage. Not that they showed it to me, and you keep quiet about me telling you this. I peeked in the window while they were all watching. If they find out, I'll get fired, and then you won't have anyone helping you out around here," she told me.

"Did you see Nick?" I asked and remembered I was talking to someone who thought he was the cat's meow, so I treaded lightly.

"Yep. He showed up with his bag of tools, and when he found her, he helped her to her feet, and you can see from the front camera that he helped her across the street like he said he did." Monica didn't tell me what I wanted to hear. "But he was here a little earlier than normal. Like an hour."

"When did the alarm go off?" I asked.

"That's the thing. The alarms didn't go off." That stopped my heart.

"Then what happened to it?" I didn't expect her to answer my question, but her statement put a lot more theories into my head.

Who could possibly have turned off the security system at the post office? Was this an inside job? I gulped.

"Monica, have you ever talked to Nick outside of work?" I asked.

"Yeah. I see a lot of people outside of work." She mentioned it so causally, I wondered what was going through her head.

"I mean, more than just casual?" I asked.

"Bernie, you're trying to be my mom again." She was certainly good at pointing that feature out. "But since I know you mean well, we did have a little something."

"A little something?" I wished she was standing in front of me, and if I'd not gotten suspended from the post office, I'd walk in there and talk to her since I was right next door, getting ready to walk into the doctor's building.

"Maybe more than a little something." Monica had a nervous sound to her voice as though she was hesitant to tell me.

"Monica..." I encouraged her in a momlike voice to tell me.

"One Sunday night after one of the summer clogging events, we were hanging out because both of us had one too many. One thing led to another, and he mentioned how it would be our little secret to go into the post office..." She didn't need to tell me anymore.

"You told him how you had a key to the post office?" I knew she had all the ins and outs on the security code, which not many employees did, including me.

"We went into the post office. The next thing I knew, I was waking up in the mail room when one of the big trucks got there from out of state. Nick was long gone." She literally just told me how Nick had access to not only watch her put in the code, but apparently, she'd fallen asleep and left him alone in there to do whatever he wanted, including taking a look at the security system.

Which, to be honest, was put in by a local company that probably anyone could hack into, including my little sweet granddaughter, Clara.

"I even deleted the film footage of us sneaking in after I came to my druthers and realized it wasn't smart to have done what we did." The sound of regret in her voice came through the phone.

I pressed the phone between my shoulder and ear as I signed my name on the clipboard next to where the receptionist sat at the doctor's office and took a seat, waiting for them to call me back.

I couldn't believe what I was hearing. Everything Monica did was not only against our company's rules but also illegal with the government.

"Please don't tell anyone, Bernie. It took me a couple of weeks to get over it and then Nick." She stopped talking and sucked in a few audible breaths. I wondered if she was trying to hold back tears. "Nick hasn't looked at me since then until today."

I looked up when I heard the door to the patient rooms open, but they called back another person. Just inside the door where patients check out, China was standing there arguing with the nurse. At least, it looked like she was fussy at the nurse.

"Listen, I've got to go. I'll call you back. Don't say anything." Monica hung up the phone.

I got up and moved closer to the door so I could see what juicy tidbits China was mad about.

"She needs it now. Not two weeks from now." I heard China's voice and leaned on the arm of the chair to get a little closer to the door.

The nurse was very calm and trying to soothe a very upset China. "I understand Peaches is having a very hard time sleeping. It's not my place to judge where her extra sleeping pills have gone, but we are not able to prescribe her anymore sleeping pills because she had plenty to last her until her next refill."

"I don't care. She needs to sleep." Frustration came off China in waves, only escalating as she talked. "She's been accused and taken into custody for murder. A murder she didn't do, and she's going to be put in a psych ward or drink herself to death if you don't give me even one pill to help her sleep. Sleep rejuvenates the brain. She needs all the brain power she can get."

"I'm going to tell you one more time, and if you don't leave after that, I'm going to call the sheriff's department to remove you." The nurse was done listening to excuses as to why Peaches didn't have any more sleeping pills.

Sleeping pills? I literally gasped out loud and then quickly shut my mouth after a few other patients looked at me. She didn't have sleeping pills because they were used on Simon.

The door of the waiting room opened, knocking me in the head.

"I'm so sorry," China gushed when she realized she'd hit someone after she'd flung the door open in a fit of rage, but she didn't actually see who it was. There was a look of shock on her face when she noticed it was me. "Bernadette." Her mouth flew open, and she knelt down.

I held my hand to my head.

"Are you okay?"

I waved her concern away.

"I'm fine." I rubbed my head a little.

"Are you sure?" she asked, voice laced with concern.

"Yes." I nodded, but upon further inspection, I could feel a little knot forming underneath my fingertip. "It's all good. You okay?"

"No." Her eyebrows dipped into a frown. "I'm here for Corine, Peaches's mom. She wants Peaches to sleep, and all her sleeping pills are gone. We don't know if she took them, sold them, or what, but she needs sleep. I thought I could get a refill on her bottle." She handed me the bottle. "No such luck."

I took notice of the name on the bottle. I would check with Vita if Barron, the coroner, had identified exactly what sleeping pills Simon had overdosed on, though we knew someone put bourbon in his mouth to make it look like he drank himself to death after writing a note saying he took the pills with a handle of bourbon, despite there being no bourbon in his system.

"I would offer you any if I had some." I handed the bottle back to her.

"Thanks, Bernadette. You've already been such a big help." Her look of concern turned to inquisitive. "Are you sick?"

"No. I have a few things I need to discuss with Dr. Hunter." The door opened again, and this time the nurse looked to make sure she didn't hit anyone.

"Bernie, you can come on back." She swiveled her gaze to China.

"I'm leaving." China put her hands in the air. "I guess I'll see you at Corine's soon? She told Peaches you were stopping by."

"Yes. See you soon." I nodded and followed the nurse back to where she not only took my weight but told me I'd gained. And just a few minutes ago, I thought my belly seemed a little smaller.

There was nothing that'd sour a mood more than when someone told you that you gained weight.

Grumpy and now with a headful of questions about where Peaches's sleeping pills disappeared to, though they probably were the ones in Simon's stomach, I was ready to get out of here before Doctor Hunter even walked in with her fifty-something self, looking put together and the picture of health.

"Hey, Bernie," Doctor Hunter greeted when she walked in. She had her gray hair flowing behind her. She tucked a strand behind her ear as she opened my chart and took a gander at it.

Though Faith was my age and we'd grown up together, she let her hair grow out gray when she was in her mid-thirties, which was well before it'd become a thing. She rocked it too. With her hip style and bright smile, Faith was able to make a sack dress cute.

"What brings you in?" She sat down next to me in the open chair.

I didn't sit on the table. There was no sense in messing up the perfectly nice piece of construction paper or whatever it was they had patients sit or lay down on when there was nothing wrong with me.

"I'm here for Barb's peace of mind." My words brought a smile to Faith's face.

"Yeah. She called, and I had to entertain her since I owe her a favor. She let me use the common room at the nursing home under their name for my Botox clinic a few weeks back." She let out a little snort. "Your parents think I'm doing some sort of back alley makeover scheme when I'm really teaching how to do Botox injections for clients with migraines." She stood up and grabbed the blood pressure cuff out of the wire basket hanging on the wall and Velcroed it on my bicep. She pumped the ball and talked, cutting off my blood circulation. "I overheard them telling one of the residents how they couldn't tell what I was doing in there. Top secret doctor stuff."

"I'm sorry." I apologized for my overbearing parents.

"No. They are cute and fine. And by the looks of your blood pressure, you are too." She tilted her head, smiling sweetly and taking the cuff off my arm while looking as cute as she did. "I heard from a certain Barbara that you're still having menopause issues. Fainting. Dizziness. Bloating, by the looks of the scale."

She flipped my chart open again, and I could tell she was scanning the page for my weight.

"No matter what I do, I can't seem to sleep, even when you suggested yoga. I did the knitting thing a few months ago, and that was disastrous." I was so embarrassed when I'd tried to knit Grady and Julia a baby blanket for Clara along with a few dishrags, and they turned out to be tiny little towels.

"Sometimes those natural things do not work, and we have to go on hormones." She frowned like she was disappointed in telling me that when we both knew it was coming, and we both knew she was very good at playing up the empathetic doctor thing.

She reached over and plucked a few brochures out of the acrylic wall hangings and handed me a few.

"Thank you. I'll take a look at these when I get a moment and let you know what I decide." This was a big decision to go on hormones and one not to be taken lightly.

I'd heard a few things, true or not, but enough to get my attention, about how taking hormones had been linked to cancer and various other diseases. Plus, I'd also heard how once you start, you can't get off them so easily.

"From what I understand, you have plenty of time on your hands." She wasn't letting me off the hook so easy.

"My mom has a big mouth." I knew Mom had told her about me passing out, then losing my mind when I accused Nick Kirby of killing Simon. None of it looked too sane.

"And why don't you read up on this too." She handed me another brochure on stress and midlife crisis.

"I'm not having a midlife crisis." I was sure of that.

"Of course, you aren't, but all stress can play into menopause." She was so sweet in her delivery that I wished she'd been a little more condescending. "If we can get your stress under control, then maybe we can get you sleeping."

After she'd gone over a few more things about my sleep, hot flashes, gut issues, and other unmentionables that didn't seem right going over with your high school classmate, we finally got on the topic of Peaches Partin.

"I know Peaches was taking pills to sleep. I was thinking of maybe getting some of those to, you know, help me sleep." I shrugged.

"Your sleeping issue is different than Peaches. Not everyone is the same, Bernie."

"I'm just afraid if I take one too many, I might not wake up, and I sure want to wake up for Clara." I was trying to figure out how many were needed to knock someone out.

"That Clara. She's a doll baby." She held her hand out for me to shake. "It was good seeing you, and I look forward to hearing what you think about the reading material I'm sending home with you."

"That's it? You're not even going to entertain my idea of needing a sleeping pill?" I asked.

"Bernadette, you forget that we went to school together. Remember when we went to the party at that old farm and the boys brought all the beer?" Looks and a good memory? Dang, Faith had it all. "You took one sip of beer and puked all night, saying you were drunk. I don't ever recall seeing a beer in your hand at a party since."

"I drink beer." I did. Rarely, but I did.

"Let's just say that if I gave you a sleeping pill, you'd be trying to throw it up a second after swallowing it." She shook a finger. "I know you. And you need to trust your doctor."

"You're the only doctor in town," I said after she shut the door so she didn't hear me.

CHAPTER 15

With a handful of no help, I headed straight back to the house on Little Creek Road. I'd passed the duck who'd been waiting for me to throw some duck pellets but realized they'd taken my mail carrier bag from me when they'd hauled me down to the post office and had me sign off on my suspension.

"I'll bring some over before I leave," I told my duck friend, who greeted me with a few quacks. "Yeah, I feel like a quack." I headed over the bridge on my dead-end side of Little Creek Road and straight toward my house.

Out of the corner of my eye, I could see the Front Porch Ladies were gathered on Millie Barnes's front porch. It was no coincidence either. Millie's house was the closest to mine, and when I didn't deliver their mail, I'm sure they were all over it. Thank goodness I made it inside before they yelled for me to stop by.

There wasn't any information to give them, and even though I really wanted to know what Millie had found out as well as Harriette when she took the repast food over to Simon Little's parents, it would have to wait.

I would have barely enough time to make it out to Peaches's parents' house before I had to come home and get ready for my super-secret date with Mac, though I wasn't supposed to know about it.

Buster greeted me at the door, his tail thudding against the table I had sitting just to the right of the door. Instead of letting him dance and prance around to give me kisses, I let him straight out to potty and went inside to check on Rowena.

She barely lifted her head to see I was home when I found her on my pillow curled up away from any sort of sunlight in the house. She loved it dark and cold on warm summer days like today.

"Hey girl," I sang out to her after she yawned, outstretched her front paws, and then arched her back as she got her footing. "Want a treat?"

It was funny how she and Buster received the word "treat" so differently. She lifted her paw and licked it a few times as if she were thinking she'd be so kind as to grace me with her presence and even accept a treat.

I heard Buster scratching at the bottom metal part of the screen door and hurried back down the hall before he got his claws on the actual screen, which I'd really gotten good at replacing over the past few months.

No wonder Mr. Macum, Buster's previous owner, didn't have a lick of screen in the screen door. He kept it taken off, and I now knew why.

"You want a treat?" I asked Buster.

Here was the difference between him and Rowena. His ears perked up. His tail did whirly twirls, and he darted into the kitchen, only to run back to see if I was coming and quickly. He did this a couple of times before I did get into the kitchen, unscrewing the treat jar with the homemade goodies from Iris.

"There you are." I eyeballed the little feline thief as she

walked into the kitchen. "You have her to thank for this screw-top jar." It took me a few seconds to get the jar open. "If she didn't knock it over all the time and spill them out on the floor for you two to gobble up, making your stomachs upset, then I wouldn't have to put a tight lid on this thing."

Rowena sat back on her haunches and threw her hind leg up in the air, licking her thigh like she didn't care a bit what I had to say.

"You two be good while I'm gone." I put a treat up on the counter far away from reach as Buster was known a time or two to counter surf, stealing any and all things edible, not to mention horrible for him. "With no job, I can't afford to take you two to the vet. So be good."

No matter what anyone told me, I was confident these two understood exactly what I was telling them.

I opened the freezer door and looked for anything in there I could take with me to the Partins'. As a Southern gal, it was beat into your brain to never go to someone's house empty-handed, and in this case, the frozen lasagna my mom had made me a few weeks back was the perfect dish to take.

I gave the fur kids one last pat goodbye, even Rowena, and headed out the door with my head down so the Front Porch Ladies couldn't catch my eye on the way to my car.

Once safely inside and driving up the street, I gave them a great big wave, or three, when I passed them. All four of them were standing up waving me to stop. The more they waved at me, the bigger my wave got.

"Shew," I said and looked in my rearview mirror at them with their hands placed on their hips and their lips moving a mile a minute, no doubt talking about me. "That was close."

Once I'd turned down Main Street and headed out of town toward Peaches's house, I let my mind wonder about the questions I needed her to answer. Some were going to be difficult and had to do with her drinking.

The subdivision her parents lived in was very nice. The houses weren't so close together like the neighborhood behind the courthouse on my third loop. These houses were built in the sixties when neighborhoods had a little more room.

This neighborhood had an LLV mail carrier, but I wasn't sure who and obviously wasn't going to find out anytime soon.

I pulled into the driveway, and Corine must've seen me pull up from inside because she greeted me at the door.

"I brought you a lasagna made by my mom." I held it out in pride knowing they were going to love it. "It's frozen so you don't have to cook it tonight."

"Are you kidding?" Peaches called out from inside the door before she popped her head out from over her mom's shoulder. "We are putting it in right now."

"Thank you, Bernadette. You shouldn't've," Corine insisted.

"Yes, she should've." Peaches reaction made her mom blush.

"I swear I taught her better than that." Corine and I both laughed, knowing Peaches was just acting out in good gesture. "Welcome to our home."

"Yeah. I'm sorry I resisted you coming now that you brought this." Peaches's eyes grew as she peeled off the tinfoil lid. "Smack my mama, this looks good."

"You better not smack your mama." Corine winked before she headed outside to the deck, which was purely a strategic move on her end to leave me and Peaches alone.

"Go on. Ask away." Peaches turned around, and the sun flooded through the windows, allowing me to get a good look at her.

"Have you been sleeping?" I knew what China was now trying to tell the doctors when she pleaded for them to refill Peaches's prescription.

"No. Unfortunately, my sleeping pills are out." She tapped the pads of her fingers underneath her eyes. "It's a little hard to sleep when you're coming off a binge and find out that you killed your ex-boyfriend who only did good things to try to keep me off the bottle."

"Are you sure you had anything to do with it? I mean, you did ask me to look into things." I helped her with the oven when she looked all around it to turn it on. "We will put that in once the preheat is finished." I patted the counter to have her set the foil pan down.

"I hate to say it, but I probably shouldn't've asked you to waste your time. Even Tim Crouse thinks I might've blacked out and killed Simon. After all, who else would he let in after hours? Who else had the return to sender package that was taken to the post office? Who else is on the video leaving Tranquility Spa with a bottle in their hand, the same bottle at the scene? And who else was seen on the security camera at the post office?" She lifted her finger and pointed to herself. "This girl."

"But did you go all the way to the garage?" I asked. "Could you physically make it to the garage, then, in your head, formulate a plan to kill him by using your prescription?"

"There're no cameras at the garage. Since there's nothing next to it on either side, and the school and country club are too far away to see anything from their cameras, then yeah. I'm it." She gnawed on her cheek and stared into space. "I don't remember picking up a bottle that night. That's the weird thing."

"Take me through the night. Step-by-step." I encouraged her to tell me what she did remember so I could see if there were any holes in her story that I could possibly think through. It took everything in my head to completely focus on her and what she was saying.

"I had an afternoon class. I was cleaning up, and the last thing I remember was seeing the return to sender package. I looked into the basket on the counter, and the mail you'd delivered that morning was there, and I wondered why you didn't take the package." She stopped and blinked a few times. "That's all I remember."

"You don't remember anything after that?" I asked, knowing that wasn't much to sleuth on or even help get her off the hook. The oven beeped, letting us know it'd reached cooking temperature.

"Not a thing." She curled up onto the balls of her feet and reached across the island to retrieve her water bottle. "I hope they have good water in jail," she teased, shaking the Tranquility Spa bottle back and forth. "I've been thinking I might be able to get them to let me teach my fellow inmates yoga."

I walked over and put the lasagna in. I punched in the timer so I'd be able to keep an eye on it.

"I'm sorry." I turned around and gave Peaches a hug like I would Grady. "I'm sorry I'm treating you like a mom, but my heart is breaking for you because you are the kindest person I know."

"You look tired, Bernie." Leave it to Peaches to put herself on the back burner when it came to noticing things about people she cared about.

"Stop worrying about me. I'm worried about you." I had to be honest with her about what I'd found. "I'm not sure I can help you. Every time I get a lead or hear a clue, it all comes back to you."

"Like what?"

"Well, we already mentioned the bourbon bottle. But did you hear he had bourbon in his mouth?" I asked, knowing Angela would die if she knew I told any sort of information she'd given me, regardless of whether she'd already asked Peaches or not.

"That can't be. Simon didn't drink bourbon. He's gluten intolerant." She looked at me.

"Yeah. Which makes me know you didn't do it. If you really killed him, you wouldn't be coherent enough to even think to put all those sleeping pills in his sports drink, then after he died, fill his mouth with bourbon. Then write a note. Whoever killed him had no idea he would be allergic to gluten." It was our only leg to stand on, and by the look on her face, she knew it too.

"How did you find all this out?" she questioned me.

"That doesn't matter. What matters is that you need to tell Tim Crouse he needs all the records from the sheriff's department, which he can get because he's your lawyer." If she told Tim what I said word-for-word, he'd not be happy.

"How can I thank you?" She threw her arms around me. "You are a genius. I told Mom that. I told China that."

"Speaking of China." This was where things got a little sketchy. "Do you think the killer took your pills?"

Her mouth dropped.

"Bernie," she gasped. "Who do you think the killer is?"

"I think it's Nick and maybe Sarah." That gave her pause. "Let me explain."

I quickly told her about me overhearing Nick and Sarah's conversation.

"I think she and Nick are having an affair, or she was going to get some sort of money out of the deal from Nick if she got information from Simon. But I can't stop seeing Nick's face when he noticed the certified letter to Simon was from the patent department and his name was not on it."

"This is starting to make a lot of sense." She blinked several times. "Nick and Sarah continued to try to see me at the studio. Nick kept telling me to listen to him, and Sarah kept trying to come to class. I left my pills at the studio, and they are gone. The only thing left was the pill bottle. I found Nick behind my counter."

"You need to tell Tim this." I knew it was probably too dangerous for me to confront Nick or Sarah at this point. So, having Tim do it and letting Angela know was probably the best thing.

Or maybe I'd give Angela a call to let her know.

"Are you okay?" I knew it was time to stop talking about the investigation. Her shoulders had slowly crept up toward her ears. Her brows were in a permanent furrow along with the lines on her forehead. Her jaw had tensed. I could see stress was written on her face.

"I need to think clearly. The only thing that helps me do that is yoga."

My heart nearly jumped into my throat when I thought she was going to say that having a drink was the only thing that helped clear her mind.

"You look like you could use some deep breathing too." The sweet disposition that I knew of hers was now shining through. There was light in her eyes when she talked about yoga that told me she was right. She needed her practice. "I can see by the dark circles you aren't getting sleep."

"No sleep because of this darn menopause," I growled, putting a smile on her face.

"I have an idea." She looked right and then left as if she didn't want her mom to hear. "You and Iris meet me at the studio tonight after ten. That way you can do your special date with Mac and my parents will be fast asleep, making it much easier for me to leave the house. We can do an hour of yoga."

"I'm worried you won't be able to resist the temptation of going to get liquor." I knew this was the time to be so honest that it might ruin the friendship we had or even our business friendship.

But I had nothing to lose on the business side. I had no idea if I was going to get my job back after the suspension or not. It was a gamble I was going to take to make sure Peaches needed what she needed to get herself clean and sober.

"I promise. I'm on a mission to find out who the real killer is and who is framing me for a murder I didn't commit. If that means getting the help I need and staying sober, I'm all for it." She pulled out a card from the back pocket of her jeans. "This is my sponsor's card, and I'll keep it with me. I've done this once. I can do it again."

There were a few moments of hesitation and a few times she gave me puppy dog eyes that melted my heart, but when she put her hands up in a prayer position and frowned at me... that did me in.

CHAPTER 16

"Hunter-green short-sleeved shirt and your black linen... um... not linen. Jeans and tennis shoes." Iris started our conversation off with an outfit.

"Huh?" I wasn't sure what on earth she was referring to.

"Your outfit for tonight. You're calling about what to wear, right?" She was so much more into this surprise than I was.

"No. I'm calling about yoga." It was like my brain hadn't processed what she'd told me to wear. "Jeans? Tennis shoes? Is he taking me on a picnic?"

"Yoga? What about yoga?" she answered me.

"First, tell me what I'm doing tonight because I wasn't going to wear jeans." I had planned on wearing a summer dress because it helped with my current hot flashes. Jeans wouldn't be good to the sweaty creases in my legs. "Did you forget I've got my own personal furnace flipped on high all day long? And in the heat of the summer night, I'm thinking no jeans."

"Just wear some sort of pants to be comfortable." She huffed. "Now that I've answered your question, you answer mine about yoga."

"I stopped by the diner after I was suspended from the post

office." While I got around to answering her question, Iris was doing a whole lot of un-hun and mmm-yea. "I ran into Corine Partin, Peaches's mom."

"Really?" Iris was intrigued. "Make this quick because I've got some pies in the oven that cannot overbake and talking on the phone with you makes me forget all about the pies."

"Fine." I was going to try to make it quick because I'd just pulled in to my house and had to get a quick shower before Mac picked me up, which was soon. "Corine asked me to stop by and talk to Peaches after she got home from being interrogated again by Angela. I did, and I think we might have some more digging around to do with Nick and Sarah. I think they both had something to do with Simon's murder. Mac said we'd be home by nine tonight, so meet me at the bakery at nine-thirty so we can go over the clues. Plus, I told Peaches that you and I would meet her at Tranquility Wellness for yoga at ten."

"PM?" Iris whined.

"Yes. She's very tense, and I think it'd do her a world of good to do some yoga over drinking." I knew Iris couldn't resist a lost soul like Peaches when I threw in the drinking part.

"Fine." In the background, I heard Iris's oven timer go off. "I've got to go. Jeans. Or pants. Just be comfortable."

She hung up, and I rushed into the house, running around doing my normal nightly routine. Give Buster some love. Let Buster out the front door. Go find Rowena and entice her with her supper while I filled up Buster's bowl with kibble. Give them both fresh water to drink, then let Buster in so he could eat while I went to get a shower and Rowena stood on the sink, watching me get ready.

After I'd held the dress and the jeans up side by side, I decided Iris wouldn't tell me wrong and pulled the jeans on, sucking in to button them. I'd not worn the jeans since early spring, and it was too soon to wear shorts. My mail carrier pants were already a little big, so they fit fine.

"Knock, knock," Mac called through the screen door on the front porch.

"Come on in!" I yelled out the bedroom door and took one last look in my mirror, running my fingers through my hair before I finally just knew there wasn't much more I could do to myself. "Here goes nothing." I gave Rowena a good scratch under her chin and headed down the hall.

Mac and Buster were sitting on the couch in the family room.

"I love you in that green color." Mac wasn't the first person who told me how much my auburn hair and skin tone went well with any shade of green. "And I'm glad you are in jeans."

"Thanks." I didn't tell him how Iris had told me what to wear because he would assume she told me what we were doing. "Are you ready?"

"I've been waiting for this moment all day." He grinned and sat on the couch like a big bump on a log.

"Let's go." I waved and gestured my head at the same time so we could leave just as I heard the front screen door open. "Grady." The excitement to see Grady put a huge smile on my face.

He held the door for Julia to come in with baby Clara nestled in the pumpkin carrier.

"We are going to have to wait a few minutes to leave." I turned and assured Mac so he wouldn't get up to go on our secret date.

"Mom," Grady said, looking down at me with his amazing big eyes, one of the many features I adored about him. "This is your big surprise."

"I love having y'all here. Especially Maw-maw's baby girl." With a smoochy face, I gushed over baby Clara.

"I don't think you understand." Julia clicked the pumpkin seat handle into the back position and unsnapped Clara, taking her out and handing her to me. "Mac has arranged it for me and Grady to go out of town since it is our anniversary, and baby Clara is going to stay with you. Originally, she was going to stay the night with you, and your parents were going to keep her during the day at the diner until you got off work, but now that you're on a leave of absence from the post office, you can spend all your free time cuddling."

"Really?" I bounced like a little kid. I'd yet to keep Clara overnight. I'd babysat here and there for a couple hours at most.

"Yes, and when we get back from our trip, we need to discuss some sort of childcare arrangement because Doctor Hunter finally cleared me to go back to work after my blood work had come back all normal." Julia was full of good news.

"Thank you." I kissed Julia. "Thank you." I made my way over to Grady. "Thank you." I gave Mac the biggest kiss of all.

"I told you this would make her happy." Mac was so pleased with himself.

"You make me happy." I gulped back the tears.

"So, does this mean you two are an item again?" Grady asked cautiously.

"It means that your mom and I decided that we are much better together than apart. We love you and you and especially you." He made baby gurgles at Clara, who was nestled in the crook of my arms, her big bright eyes staring at me.

She smiled.

"Did you see that?" I gushed. "Your maw-maw loves you." I kept repeating that to her because she kept smiling at me. "She's so smart. She already knows my voice."

"Okay, Mom"—Grady had a sarcastic tone in his voice—"Don't be like all grandmothers and think Clara will ever do no wrong, because she will at one point."

"No, she won't. She's too much of a little angel for such nonsense." I refused to believe my precious Clara would ever get into any sort of trouble.

"Don't argue with the grandmother," Mac warned with a grin. "You two get out of here and don't you worry about a thing."

Mac had gotten up and walked a very nervous-looking Julia to the door. Her head continued to be turned past her shoulder with her eyes on Clara.

"We've got this." Mac continued to assure her.

"Are you sure?" Julia appeared to be changing her mind. "I mean, it's been quite a long time since there's been a baby in the family."

"It's been quite a long time since I've been alone with my wife." Grady grabbed her hand. "Clara is fine. We need this time."

"You're right." Julia nodded and looked back at me and Clara. "One more kiss."

She hurried over, like a good mama, and gave me a warm hug and kissed Clara goodbye.

"Thank you, Maw-maw." Julia's face lit up clear into the depths of her eyes. "You're the best."

"You two go have fun," I told them and laughed after they'd left and I heard them giggling on the way out to their truck.

Mac had followed them outside and waved them off from the front porch.

"Mac Tabor, you always know what I want," I told him when he walked back in. "Get over here and give me a kiss."

When he leaned a little too close, I put my hand up on his chest.

"Careful." I warned him not to squish Clara.

"I see her." His little grin stayed on his lips when he leaned in a little more to kiss me. "I've completely lost you for the entire weekend. What have I done?"

"You've made me the happiest person in the entire world." I looked down at my grandbaby in awe and let the joy fill my heart.

I was very blessed before Clara, but Clara made me feel doubly blessed and grateful.

Mac had thought of everything. Down to the supper my parents had delivered from the diner.

"Now you know how it feels to just love something so unconditionally." My mom barely ate because she held Clara the entire time and didn't take an eye off of her.

It was so enduring seeing my mom holding my grandbaby. It was a moment that would be tattooed in my memory forever.

The night seemed to flow by so quickly. I feared the few days I had with Clara would do the same. These were hours I would cherish, and I knew how important my role was in her life.

"Do you think I should just quit instead of keeping the suspension?" I asked Mac after I'd fed and put Clara down for the night.

Dusk was starting to settle and a few fireflies batted around the air while we enjoyed the summer night breeze from the rocking chairs on the front porch. Buster was lying on the top step, and Rowena was sitting at the screen door.

"I think you need to do what you want. You don't have to worry about your retirement because I'll always take care of you." He didn't look at me when he said it. He simply stared ahead and rocked back and forth.

"I know you will." I could've kept my mouth shut, but like any person, he needed to hear me say the words out loud. "I also know that you support me and Grady. Julia too."

"Bernie, I consider Clara as much my granddaughter as you do." He finally looked at me with tears in his eyes. "You have no idea the relief you've given me the last couple of days. Over the past few months, I've been a broken man. I've been trying to change who I've been over these last thirty-something years since I met you from Richard. I didn't ever get married because of my feelings for you. It was not right to do to another woman. I could never love another woman the way I loved you, and I never wanted to lie to anyone I would've married out of knowing I'd never have you." His chest heaved up as he sucked in a breath, attempting to gather his feelings. "I'd rather be single my whole life if I can't be right here like I am now. Seeing you this happy makes life worth living."

He gently reached over across the rocking chairs and laid his hand on mine.

"No matter what the future holds. Friends. Companions. Or more than that. Simply being with you like this right now is enough for my entire lifetime."

"Mac"—I had to say his name before I responded to him and get my dry mouth wet—"what you've done tonight means more to me than anything you could ever give me. I..."

"There you are!" Harriette Pearl yelled from the bridge across the street from my house. "Did you forget about us baking at Pie in the Face?"

"What time is it?" I jerked my head and looked at Mac.

"Almost nine-thirty. Why?" He moved his gaze back and forth between me and Harriette, who was now waving me over like a parent calling me to come in before dark.

"I had no idea what you were planning, but you told me I'd be home by nine. I made plans to bake with Iris and..." I swallowed down the lie. "Harriette."

I had no idea why Harriette was there, and I knew I'd find out soon enough.

"Iris didn't tell me anything, so I'm..."

"Off the hook. I only thought we were going to get to babysit for Grady and Julia so they could go to supper to celebrate their anniversary. It was after you got suspended that I came up with the idea to send them off for the weekend. I knew it would make you happy and give them some much needed time away."

"So I can go? I mean, I'm just across the street, and I'll be back by eleven." I figured yoga with Peaches, which I didn't tell him about, would be over way before eleven, so it was a good time to tell him I'd be back. "And Clara is asleep; Julia says she sleeps all night now."

"Go. I've got Buster and Rowena to keep me company the next few hours." He gave a quick nod of his chin.

"I'll be right there, Harriette!" I yelled back to her after I noticed she was shuffling over the bridge toward the house.

I got up, walked in front of Mac, and leaned down.

"Are you giving me a kiss?" he asked.

"This time Harriette isn't going to interrupt." I kissed him gently on the lips.

CHAPTER 17

"Normally, I wouldn't interrupt such an intimate moment, but we've got people's lives at stake here." Harriette scolded me all the way to the bakery. "According to Simon's mother, he was deliberately murdered and by someone he knew."

"What did she say?" I was curious to hear what Angela had been telling Simon's family about his murder.

I swung the door of the bakery open and let Harriette go in before me. Harriette continued to babble on about how much they appreciated her bringing the casserole over and how wonderful and kind she was to remember them in their grief.

"What's all this about?" I looked at Ruby, Gertrude, Millie, and Iris sitting around the prep station when we finally made it back to the kitchen.

"We are testing out this summer sausage casserole Iris threw together for us to munch on." Ruby Dean was very excited over any food.

"How did y'all know we were coming to bake?" I gave Iris the stink eye.

"Is that code for decipherin' all the clues you found today?"

Millie Barnes looked up at me. "Because if this is how y'all do it, I'll just be of no use because once my belly gets full, my eyes get heavy."

"Then we better get to it." Iris had already erased all the custom orders she kept up on the whiteboard and replaced customers' names with Simon Little in a big circle in the middle. With all the offshoots, she made it look like a big sun with rays coming from it.

Peaches Partin was written on one of the rays, Sarah Hodges on another, followed by Nick Kirby. Sadly, the rest were left empty.

"The facts are as follows," I began to read while Iris wrote things down. "Simon Little was found dead with a bottle of bourbon sitting on his desk, an empty prescription bottle on the ground, and a written note on his computer to make it all appear as a self-inflicted death. But upon further investigation and a preliminary autopsy report, Simon Little only had a deep purple sports drink in his stomach along with a lethal amount of sleeping pills. Simon Little's mouth had bourbon in it like someone had taken the bourbon and poured it into his mouth.

"So, we know that Peaches not only dated Simon for a long period of time, but he knew about her drinking problem. Her bottle of bourbon was found at the scene, along with a package she took to the post office. And somehow, she got it back after-hours. She's on camera walking from Tranquility Spa to the post office then passing out."

I gave the items for Iris to write down very clearly so none of the Front Porch Ladies could stop me by asking me to repeat myself.

"Peaches also knows that Simon is allergic to gluten, which can be found in some bourbons, and Simon stayed away from alcohol. Peaches told me that Nick and Sarah have both been to Tranquility Spa, where she kept her sleeping pills and had that bourbon bottle. Not only did she find Nick behind the shop counter, but she also noticed her pills were missing from the bottle."

My words were met with shocked expressions.

"Sarah Hodges and Nick Little were arguing at the gas station when I showed up there to do a little questioning, and I heard them with my own ears, and I quote." I looked at Iris to make sure she'd caught up with me while writing it all down. She gave me the go ahead. "They were talking about stealing the final plans of someone who was alive and is now dead." The details were sketchy, but I got the gist of it. "They talked about how they could move on with their lives. And I can only think it was because of the patent Simon had gotten for the motorcycle part they'd designed."

"That's what Simon's mom was talking about," Harriette said, chiming in, "she said Simon had been very excited before he'd gone back to the garage that night because he had gotten the final 3D product and was going to meet up with Nick to get it on the bike to test it out. She also mentioned the patent he'd filed had come in, and he couldn't wait until the morning to have the mail carrier deliver it."

"Which brings me back to Nick. He was also seen on the post office security video camera with Peaches. Right?" Gertrude asked.

"Right. And Monica Reed told me that he'd shown up earlier than normal that morning and was with her the entire time she called the sheriff about the break-in, and he never mentioned once he'd been there already with Peaches." It was like we all had the same idea.

"Do you think Nick set Peaches up? I mean, on paper, she does look like the killer." Gertrude kept throwing out theories that all made sense and placed Nick at the scene.

"His mom did say he was meeting Nick at the station." Gertrude reiterated what Mrs. Little had said.

"And Nick did have access to Peaches's bourbon bottle and pills if he took her back, if not before, when she caught him behind the counter." Millie nudged Ruby, who poked Gertrude, who smacked Harriette on the arm.

Iris finished writing everything we said or threw out on the board. The click of the top of the dry-erase marker made us all jump when she popped it on. Iris took a step back from the board and crossed her arms across her body.

All of us stared at the board as though we were rereading what we'd said. If they were anything like me, they were playing the scene over in their head.

"Ladies," I said, addressing them. "I think we just solved Simon Little's murder."

All of us looked around. None of us had happy or proud faces. Sadness settled into each one of our matured faces.

After a bit of debate, we all decided we'd sleep on what we'd come up with and I'd take it all to Angela in the morning. It was already late and a Friday night. Another night wasn't going to hurt. Though I did make a note about how we needed to find out what time the autopsy believed Simon was murdered.

"Are you sure y'all are going to be okay walking home?" I asked the Front Porch Ladies as the time inched closer to ten o' clock.

It was well after dark, and I didn't want them to be in danger, though I was confident they would be fine. It was only good manners to check with them to make sure. Of course, they pish-poshed me when I even brought it up.

"Aren't you going to walk with us?" Harriette gave me the side eye.

"I'm going to help Iris clean up and walk her to her car." I shrugged, trying not to give away that we were actually going next door to do yoga. I was positive Peaches didn't need the stress of four ladies in their eighties trying to downward dog when she had this fifty-year-old broad trying her best not to break a hip moving from warrior one to warrior two pose.

"I'll drive her home." Iris gestured with her fork before she took another huge bite of the casserole.

The Front Porch Ladies all looked between each other and nodded that they were going to walk on home. Before they even left, they were already gossiping about something else other than the murder we just solved.

"I think I'll bring this to Sunday supper since Grady and Julia will be just getting home from their trip." Iris moved around the kitchen, putting away the clean dishes. "Which you never said a word about your big surprise. How was seeing Clara?"

"Seeing her? She's at my house right now. Mac had come up with the idea that Grady and Julia should go away for the weekend instead of just supper." I tried to contain the joy I was feeling since I knew there was so much more pain by so many other families in Sugar Creek Gap.

"And you want to do yoga?" Iris rolled her eyes and came at me, trying to push me out of the kitchen. "Go home and be with your grandbaby and your man."

I dug my heels in and didn't budge.

"Nope. I've got all weekend long to be hugging up on both of them. Especially Clara, who just so happens to be asleep for the night." I laughed when Iris booty bumped me. "Stop it. Come on. Let's go, we're going to be late."

"Geez, Bernie. If I didn't know better, I'd think you're really enjoying yoga." When she looked at me, I glared back at her, which made her laugh. "What's in your bag?"

"Those awful pants I'll put on just to make Peaches happy." I flung it over my shoulder and headed to the front of the bakery with Iris flipping the lights off behind me. "I'm not going to even bring up the murder."

"You don't think we should tell her our theory since she did ask you to help?" Iris had a point. She locked the front door of the bakery, and we headed next door.

"No. I don't want to get her hopes up if something is off. It's best we take our theory to Angela like I promised Angela and let her do the leg work." I knocked on the door of Tranquility Spa and was happy to see Peaches coming toward us. "Besides, if Peaches tells anyone, then Sarah and Nick could run off."

"Good thinking." Iris planted a big smile on her face, as did I, as soon as Peaches opened the door.

"Hey ladies. You two are lifesavers. I needed this tonight." Peaches looked like she was the Zen queen I'd always known her to be.

She looked calmer and a little less tense than she had a few hours earlier.

"And we need to get you sleeping." She let go of the door after I grabbed the handle and ushered Iris in. "If you two want to grab a mat and meet me in the room, we will get started. I don't want my mom to realize I've left because she will have a heart attack."

"I'll get changed real quick." I held up the bag I'd brought from home with my too tight yoga pants along with the new shirt China had made me and headed toward the bathroom where there were a couple stalls that doubled as changing rooms.

Peaches had really thought of everything when she'd redone the old building.

Iris and Peaches were waiting for me and chitchatting about what Iris could do to help with some sort of pain she was having. It was one of those aches that we brushed off, saying it just came with age. Instead of trying to hear Peaches's reply to

Iris, I tried to get in the zone as I grabbed a mat, but my head was back at my house with Clara and Mac... my world.

"Let's get started, ladies." Peaches was sitting cross-legged on her aqua mat. "We are going to start on all fours. Be sure to take in some deep breaths as we start with cat cow pose." Peaches's body was so flexible as she curled her spine up and then let her back arch as she dropped her belly. "Drop the belly and open the chest." A big exhale came from her.

Iris and I both followed her lead.

"Chin to chest and breath out. Claw through the fingertips as you draw your chin to chest." She continued the movement for a few more breaths. "Finish off that breath as we meet together in tabletop."

The cat cow felt so good to me. I didn't want to stop doing that. A big yawn came out of nowhere.

"I see you're yawning. Let it out. That means your body is relaxing." Peaches's voice was so soft and soothing. "Bump your hips to the right and gaze past your left shoulder. Come back to center and draw little circles with your tailbone forward, backward, and reverse."

Peaches continued with these easy and simple poses that made me wonder why I'd not embraced yoga in the last few classes because this was wonderful. Maybe it was the other students in class, but I now understood why Peaches would tell the class not to focus on anyone in the room but to focus on our practice. She'd tell us to listen to our bodies, not try to do what our neighbor's body was doing.

Before I knew it, the time passed, and she already had us lying in corpse pose on our mats.

"Nice and easy breaths. Close your eyes. Take a beautiful inhale through your nose, and this time, as you exhale, allow the weight of your body to relax completely and fully."

And that was the last thing I remembered until I woke

myself up snoring. I sat up straight so Iris and Peaches didn't have to nudge me and tried to pretend I hadn't fallen asleep.

"Iris? Peaches?" I twisted around on the mat to see where they'd gone. They weren't in the room at all, so I got up figuring they were in the front of Tranquility Wellness while they let me take a snoozer.

The lights were off, and the place was empty. It was crazy. There was a note taped to the front door with my name written on it.

We just had to let you sleep. You were sleeping so well that I knew you needed it. Iris called Mac to let him know you'd fallen asleep during yoga, and he said to let you sleep. If you wake up before I get here in the morning, just let yourself out the back door of the building. You can turn the lock on your way out. It's located in the storage room that is right across from meditation room 3. Hugs and happy sleeping. Peaches.

Half out of it, I took the note off the door and headed back toward the rooms she referred to as the meditation rooms. There was a thud above me, and I tilted my head to see if it was thunder. There'd not been a call for rain, though we could definitely use some if the crops this fall were going to be any good. When I heard the thump again, it sounded like mice.

I sure would hate to see Peaches have a mouse problem on top of the bank issues. A long sad sigh escaped me, but my body felt so good and relaxed I couldn't wait to get home and crawl into bed. I was going to take advantage of being on suspension and snuggle all day with Clara.

I found the door across from meditation room three and opened it, and there I found the door to the outside. I'd thought Peaches would've boarded up the back door like everyone else, but she actually had made it one of the fire exits. She was so smart.

The thump turned into a louder ticking sound before something much louder fell above me. There was a muffled talking sound.

"Peaches? Iris?" I called out and noticed a small step of stairs off to the left of the door.

There were so many times I'd walked by this building as a child and as an adult on my mail route wondering what on earth was behind the little window in the two-story building.

I clumped up the steps since I could hear someone mumbling, figuring on Iris and Peaches being up there.

"Thanks for not waking me up... again," I said after my foot landed on the top step. "Peaches!" I gasped and dropped the yoga bag with my regular clothes in it when I saw she was strapped to a chair on her side. "What in the world is going on?" I questioned and tried to remove the gag around her mouth.

Her eyes looked at me with fear in them before I realized we weren't alone.

"Now you. I knew you were going to be a problem." China Gordon was standing at the top of the steps and rolled her eyes.

CHAPTER 18

It took a minute for my sleeping eyes to adjust and notice that it was in fact China. She looked so much like Peaches that I'd have thought it was Peaches if I'd not seen her all tied up.

"The cameras. The pills. The bourbon bottle." It was like my mouth had a mind of its own, which it often did, but not when a gun was pointed directly at me. "You probably didn't know Simon wasn't a bourbon drinker."

"And here I thought you only knew how to count so you could deliver little letters to mailboxes." China tried to put me down, but I stayed laser focused on the gun and her.

"Looks like I have nothing to lose before you kill me and Peaches, so why don't I take a stab at just exactly how you pulled this off?"

"I'm listening." She appeared to be interested in what I had to say. Almost entertained.

"Can I ask a question? I need to tie up one loose end. The package."

"You've even said yourself that I look like Peaches. So I took the package for Peaches to the post office after you didn't do your job to pick it up." She didn't say anything else, which explained seeing her on the grainy camera footage since she looked like Peaches. "I'd love to hear your theory."

"I'd love to give it to you, but first, I need to know why you killed Simon." I tried so hard to take some deep breaths to calm myself, but the yoga pants were too dang tight for me to even get any comfort.

"That shirt you're wearing." She took a step closer and reached out with her free hand to flick the sleeve. "I've been trying for weeks to get Peaches to meet with me about the yoga clothing line. But she's been so upset about Simon and Sarah Hodges that I knew the only way she'd return to normal was to get rid of him."

Peaches moaned out, still lying on her side on the ground, attached to the chair. Tears streamed down her face.

I remembered the few times this week I'd seen China try to get Peaches to listen to her.

"You knew Peaches was a recovering alcoholic, so you were more than happy to have those shots of bourbon. And when I saw you at the doctor's office trying to refill her prescription, it was because you wanted to get her bottle filled up, and I bet she didn't even know you went to the doctor on her behalf." My words brought a smile to China's face and more grunts from Peaches to confirm I was right.

"Shut up!" she yelled at Peaches. "Peaches fed me lies about how I could start a clothing line and she'd help me. All these years she's been a drunk, and she's the one who comes out on top. Smelling like a rose. Be a drunk and open a successful yoga studio while I bust my rump learning web development and working for yoga companies."

"You are a web designer?" I questioned, thinking she was some sort of yoga clothing salesperson.

"Duh. How do you think I deleted all the footage of me

breaking in to the post office to get that darn package back? And the letter. The letter you had for Simon that I overheard in the doctor's office that day. Yeah. I wanted the letter, so when I got the package, it looked like he broke in to get the letter. It was too good though." She smiled. "I opened the package he sent to Peaches. There was a letter inside telling her all about how I'd come to him about some business idea I had, which I did. I wanted to open up my own studio and have my own clothing line, so I went to him for advice on how to start a business because my dear friend Peaches never shared with me anymore."

China shifted her gaze to Peaches. The moonlight shined through the small window, casting enough of a shadow on her that I could see the pure hatred on her face.

"I went to see him after I took the package to the post office. I told him she wouldn't open it, but if he helped me with my business, I could get her to open it. Maybe come back to him and sober." She snorted. "That's when he said he sent the package because he thought she'd open it since she hadn't taken any of his phone calls. Then he proceeded to tell me what was in the package and how it was a letter against me." There was so much passion in China's voice, I could hear how she believed she was in the right by killing Simon. "That's when I knew I had to break in to the post office and get the package back so I could make it look like she did it."

When she nodded to Peaches, I looked away for a second toward her. Her eyes were barely open.

"You went to see him, and somehow, you took Peaches's pills and crushed them up, knowing he would drink that sports drink." All of the evidence was becoming so clear. "You made it look like he was drinking, and you knew how to break in to his computer and write that note."

"With him gone, I would be able to get Peaches back on track and get my clothing line off the ground like she promised me." Her words made me so angry.

I continued to try to get some composure and some sort of deep breath, but my circulation was cut off by the darn pants, and deep inside me frustration began to boil.

There was nothing angrier than a middle-aged woman who was going through menopause wearing a snug pair of yoga pants.

It was like I had one good breath in me as I took off toward China with my head down as fast and hard as I could. I swung my bag with my cell phone in there, hoping to hit her in the head with it.

She grabbed the bag and took a stumble backward. I bent down and covered my head once my bag left my grip, fearing she was going to hit me with it. Shards of glass fell around me, and when I looked up, China was no longer in the room, and the window was shattered.

Slowly, I got up and carefully walked over to the window, barely leaning over enough to see China was lying on Main Street in a position that didn't look like she survived the fall.

"Peaches!" I hurried to her side and noticed she was passed out. One of her Tranquility Wellness bottles was lying on the floor next to her. I picked it up and lifted it into the moonlight. "Oh my gosh, sediment." I noticed it looked exactly like the bottle that Simon had drank out of. "She drugged you."

I left her there and hurried back downstairs since my cell phone was in the bag that'd gone out the window with China. I fumbled through the dark shop and found myself at the counter where the phone was located, but the flashing lights outside told me someone had already called the sheriff.

I ran to the door, unlocked it, and ran out.

"Peaches is upstairs. I think she's been overdosed like Simon!" I tried to say the words as clear as I could so Angela only had to get the EMTs, who just pulled up, to get up there and get her.

I stood back while she ordered who to get what. They headed inside, and she kneeled down to feel for a pulse on China.

"She's dead." Angela Hafley's words sent chills up my spine.

CHAPTER 19

The smell of a baby was the most amazing scent. There was nothing that compared. Everything was perfect on Clara, down to her cupid bow lips and button nose.

"I'm sorry I'm not helping, but I don't get nearly enough time with her." I looked around the old farmhouse kitchen while Iris and Julia worked to get Sunday supper on the table.

"You're gonna have to give up that baby and give her great-granny a dose." My mom put her hands out for me to hand Clara over. "Give 'er to me." She got grabby hands.

"Mom." I twisted around so she couldn't get her.

"You need to give her to me so you can tell us the details of what on earth happened after they took Peaches to the hospital." Mom stood up over me.

Reluctantly, I handed her over and knew this would be the only time to tell the girls about what'd happened because I didn't get my cell phone back from the sheriff's department until after they took China Gordon to the morgue.

Mac was so relieved to know I was okay but made me promise not to keep things from him. We talked all through the night about being honest and respectful, even when we didn't see eye to eye. We also agreed that if Angela Hafley had asked me to be a special consultant on any more cases, I'd be up front with him about my involvement. It was going to be a hard thing to do since I'd been so independent for so long, but Mac was important to me, and I was going to really try to honor our agreement.

"I can't believe China did it." Iris put her smoky sausage casserole dish in the middle of the table. "After I thought about seeing her at Tranquility Spa over the past few weeks during yoga, I can now see it. There were so many signs."

"So many signs." I picked the edge of a really crispy piece of casserole off the top and popped it into my mouth. I loved burnt pieces of casserole so much. "Even with the drinking. Every time after class when the bourbon bottle was out, it was always China pouring the drinks, and she made sure Peaches was getting drunk."

"Her mom said if it weren't for you, Peaches would've never agreed to go to rehab straight from the hospital after they pumped her stomach to get all those pills China forced her to drink out." Mom kept kissing Clara on the head, no doubt trying to wake the sleeping baby.

"I'm sure she's going to get back on track this time." I opened the utensil drawer and got out the silverware to put next to each place setting. Iris got out all the glasses and started to fill them with ice.

"I heard from Harriette that Nick and Sarah had started dating. Nick and Sarah were going to go over to talk to Simon about them, and they saw he was sleeping in the office. They had no idea he was already dead, so they left. They pretty much chickened out, but they have alibis before and after the time of death which ruled them out." Iris put a glass next to each plate and then poured the freshly brewed sweet tea. "She also said Nick signed a contract with Simon's mom to continue the motorcycle part patent. They are going to give Simon's earnings to the Motorcycle Safety Fund. It was near and dear to Simon's heart."

"What Nick did wasn't illegal. It was immoral." Julia walked past my mom with the salad. She put it on the table and then ran her hand over Clara's head. "She's the best baby."

"She is!" Grady and the other two men bolted through the back door.

"Shhhhh," all the women said in unison to get them to be quiet because of the sleeping baby.

"How are you?" Mac walked over to where I was standing and whispered into my ear as he put his arms around me.

"I'm actually perfect and exactly where I want to be." I turned my head far enough to kiss him on the lips. "I love you, Mac Tabor."

Want to continue your vacation in Sugar Creek Gap?
The next book in the series, FIRST CLASS KILLER is available for preorder!

RECIPES

Smoky Sausage and Grits Summer Casserole
Southern Strawberry Shortcake

SMOKY SAUSAGE AND GRITS SUMMER CASSEROLE

Ingredients

1 1/2 pounds smoked sausage, chopped
    1/2 teaspoon table salt
    1 1/2 cups uncooked quick-cooking grits
    2 (8-oz.) blocks sharp Cheddar cheese, shredded
    1 cup milk
    1 1/2 teaspoons chopped fresh thyme
    1/4 teaspoon garlic powder
    1/4 teaspoon black pepper
    4 large eggs, lightly beaten
    Vegetable cooking spray

Directions

1) Preheat oven to 350°. Brown sausage in a large skillet over medium-high heat, stirring often, 7 to 9 minutes or until cooked; drain on paper towels.

2) Bring salt and 4 1/2 cups water to a boil in a large Dutch oven

over high heat. Whisk in grits, and return to a boil. Cover, reduce heat to medium, and simmer 5 minutes or until thickened, whisking occasionally. Remove from heat; add cheese, stirring until completely melted. Stir in milk and next 4 ingredients. Stir in sausage. Spoon mixture into a lightly greased (with cooking spray) 13- x 9-inch baking dish.

3) Bake at 350° for 50 minutes to 1 hour or until golden and cooked through. Let stand 5 minutes before serving.

SOUTHERN STRAWBERRY SHORTCAKE

Ingredients

4 cups fresh strawberries, quartered
   1 tablespoon lemon zest
   2 Tbsp. fresh juice
   1/2 cup plus 2 Tbsp. granulated sugar
   divided 4 cups all-purpose flour
   1 tablespoon baking powder
   1 teaspoon baking soda
   1 1/2 teaspoon kosher salt
   1 1/4 cups cold unsalted butter, cut into small pieces
   1 1/2 cups whole buttermilk
   2 cups and 2 Tbsp. cold heavy cream
   divided 1 tablespoon coarse sugar
   1/2 cup powdered sugar
   1 vanilla bean pod, split

Directions

1) Stir together strawberries, lemon zest, lemon juice, and 1/2 cup

of the granulated sugar in a medium bowl. Cover; refrigerate at least 30 minutes or up to 1 hour.

2) Preheat oven to 425°F. Whisk together flour, baking powder, baking soda, salt, and remaining 2 tablespoons granulated sugar in a large bowl. Cut in butter with a pastry blender until mixture resembles peas. Add buttermilk, and stir gently with a spatula or wooden spoon until well combined and shaggy. Turn out dough onto a lightly floured surface, and knead gently until dough just comes together, 2 to 3 times. Pat dough with lightly floured palms to 1 1/2-inch thickness (do not use a rolling pin). Cut out biscuits using a 2 1/2-inch round cutter, gathering and patting scraps once more to make 12 biscuits.

3) Place biscuits about 2 inches apart on a parchment paper-lined baking sheet. Refrigerate 30 minutes. Brush tops of biscuits with 2 tablespoons of the heavy cream; sprinkle with sugar. Bake in preheated oven until golden brown, 18 to 20 minutes. Cool on baking sheet 10 minutes.

4) Place powdered sugar in bowl of an electric stand mixer fitted with whisk attachment. Scrape vanilla bean seeds into powdered sugar; add remaining 2 cups heavy cream. Beat on medium speed until soft peaks form, 4 to 5 minutes. Split biscuits; place on plates or a large platter. Spoon strawberry mixture onto bottom halves of biscuits. Dollop with whipped cream; cover with biscuit tops.

Like this book?
Tap here to leave a review now!
Join Tonya's newsletter to stay updated with new releases, get free novels, access to exclusive bonus content, and more!

Join Tonya's newsletter here.
Tap here to see all of Tonya's books.
Join all the fun on her Reader Group on Facebook.

Also By Tonya Kappes

Magical Cures Mystery Series
A CHARMING CRIME
A CHARMING CURE
A CHARMING POTION (novella)
A CHARMING WISH
A CHARMING SPELL
A CHARMING MAGIC
A CHARMING SECRET
A CHARMING CHRISTMAS (novella)
A CHARMING FATALITY
A CHARMING DEATH (novella)
A CHARMING GHOST
A CHARMING HEX
A CHARMING VOODOO
A CHARMING CORPSE
A CHARMING MISFORTUNE
A CHARMING BLEND (CROSSOVER WITH A KILLER COFFEE COZY)

A Camper and Criminals Cozy Mystery
BEACHES, BUNGALOWS, & BURGLARIES
DESERTS, DRIVERS, & DERELICTS
FORESTS, FISHING, & FORGERY
CHRISTMAS, CRIMINALS, & CAMPERS
MOTORHOMES, MAPS, & MURDER
CANYONS, CARAVANS, & CADAVERS
ASSAILANTS, ASPHALT, & ALIBIS
VALLEYS, VEHICLES & VICTIMS
SUNSETS, SABBATICAL, & SCANDAL
TENTS, TRAILS, & TURMOIL

Also By Tonya Kappes

Killer Coffee Mystery Series
SCENE OF THE GRIND
MOCAH AND MURDER
FRESHLY GROUND MURDER
COLD BLOODED BREW
DECAFFEINATED SCANDAL
A KILLER LATTE
HOLIDAY ROAST MORTEM
DEAD TO THE LAST DROP
A CHARMING BLEND NOVELLA (CROSSOVER WITH MAGICAL CURES MYSTERY)

Mail Carrier Cozy Mystery
STAMPED OUT
ADDRESS FOR MURDER
ALL SHE WROTE
RETURN TO SENDER

A Ghostly Southern Mystery Series
A GHOSTLY UNDERTAKING
A GHOSTLY GRAVE
A GHOSTLY DEMISE
A GHOSTLY MURDER
A GHOSTLY REUNION
A GHOSTLY MORTALITY
A GHOSTLY SECRET
A GHOSTLY SUSPECT

A Southern Cake Baker Series
(WRITTEN UNDER MAYEE BELL)
CAKE AND PUNISHMENT
BATTER OFF DEAD

Kenni Lowry Mystery Series
FIXIN' TO DIE
SOUTHERN FRIED
AX TO GRIND
SIX FEET UNDER
DEAD AS A DOORNAIL
TANGLED UP IN TINSEL
DIGGIN' UP DIRT

Spies and Spells Mystery Series
SPIES AND SPELLS
BETTING OFF DEAD
GET WITCH or DIE TRYING

A Laurel London Mystery Series
CHECKERED CRIME
CHECKERED PAST
CHECKERED THIEF

A Divorced Diva Beading Mystery Series
A BEAD OF DOUBT SHORT STORY
STRUNG OUT TO DIE
CRIMPED TO DEATH

Olivia Davis Paranormal Mystery Series
SPLITSVILLE.COM
COLOR ME LOVE (novella)
COLOR ME A CRIME

ABOUT TONYA

Tonya has written over 65 novels, all of which have graced numerous bestseller lists, including the USA Today. *Best known for stories charged with emotion and humor and filled with flawed characters, her novels have garnered reader praise and glowing critical reviews. She lives with her husband and a very spoiled rescue cat named Ro. Tonya grew up in the small southern Kentucky town of Nicholasville. Now that her four boys are grown men, Tonya writes full-time.*

Learn more about her books here. Find her on Facebook, Twitter, BookBub, and her website.

Sign up to receive her newsletter, where you'll get free books, exclusive bonus content, and news of her releases and sales.

If you liked this book, please take a few minutes to leave a review now! Authors (Tonya included) really appreciate this, and it helps draw more readers to books they might like. Thanks!

This book is a work of fiction. The characters, incidents, and dialogue are drawn from the author's imagination and are not to be construed as real. Any resemblance to actual events or persons, living or dead, is entirely coincidental. The cover was made by Mariah Sinclair. Red Edit Publishing for edits.

Copyright © 2020 by Tonya Kappes. All rights reserved. Printed in the United States of America. No part of this book may be used or reproduced in any manner whatsoever without written permission except in the case of brief quotations embodied in critical articles and reviews. For information email Tonyakappes@tonyakappes.com

Made in the USA
Monee, IL
08 November 2020